D0595911

THE TIGER IN MEN

When Fenella Shaw left England to take possession of a Canadian cattle ranch in the Saskatchewan Valley, gifted to her as a legacy by her father, she quickly fell in love with handsome Max Geerling, the manager. It came as no surprise to anyone when the news of their engagement was announced, the neighbouring farmers believing them to be ideally matched. But Max is not all he seems to be — and Fenella finds herself caught up in a situation so alien to her that she fears she may never escape . . .

DENISE ROBINS

THE TIGER
IN MEN

Complete and Unabridged

LINFORD
Leicester

First published in Great Britain in 1969 by
Arrow Books Ltd.
London

First Linford Edition
published 2014
by arrangement with
Arrow Books Ltd.
London

A catalogue record for this book is available
from the British Library.

ISBN 978–1–4448–2083–6

Published by
F. A. Thorpe (Publishing)
Anstey, Leicestershire

Set by Words & Graphics Ltd.
Anstey, Leicestershire
Printed and bound in Great Britain by
T. J. International Ltd., Padstow, Cornwall

This book is printed on acid-free paper

1

Fenella stood on the porch of her bungalow, looked out at the night, and thought it was one of the loveliest she had ever seen.

It was March, and out here, twenty miles south of Edmonton, Alberta, March meant the end of the long, cold winter, and the breaking through of the spring.

To the lonely ranchers spring signifies the renewal of hope. The growing of young green things, the shooting of the tender wheat, the bursting into blossom of the trees in the vast forests, and the thawing of the ice on the rivers. The end of hardships and the beginning of soft, lovely days, when the dead grass comes to life, and the poplars and the birches show their green, and the great white, wild geese fly across the lakes to seek their nesting-grounds.

To Fenella Shaw, this was a very particular spring. A season of rapture for her, unlike any other in her life.

It was the first spring she had known out here in the Saskatchewan Valley, for she had only come from England at the end of the autumn last year to take possession of this cattle ranch which had been her father's legacy.

Tonight she looked with tender, speculative eyes across the fertile acres and grazing-fields which belonged to her, and away to the distant mountain peaks which were still glittering white with snow in the March moonlight.

There had been a time when she had first come out to Canada when she had felt she could never grow used to the strange, hard life which she had to lead. So different from the civilised existence of England in a London flat, and of the first twenty years of her life spent with a mother who thought of nothing but playing bridge and educating her daughter to attract a husband of means.

During those twenty years Fenella

had not been unhappy, although always conscious that she was in a *milieu* foreign to her nature. She had missed her father. He and her mother had separated while she was still a babe. Dick Shaw had never cared for a conventional existence, nor for the frivolities which meant the breath of life to his pleasure-loving Irish wife.

Finally he had bought himself a ranch in Canada and remained there. It had flourished, and he duly sent home the necessary money to support his wife and child, but never returned to them.

Mrs. Shaw's death of septic pneumonia left Fenella alone in the world except for this father whom she had never known and with whom she immediately communicated. After her mother's funeral, he cabled for her to join him in Alberta.

Fenella had sailed away from England without many regrets. She had always wanted to lead an open-air life. She preferred horses and dogs and the country to the London which her poor mother had adored. She had come through the last two years of this 'social round' without losing her heart to any of the men who lost theirs for Fenella. Fenella, who was slim and lovely, full of an unconscious grace and the charm of smoke-grey eyes bequeathed to her by Ireland, dark brows and lashes, and hair the colour of wheat with the sun on it.

But she had more than that haunting beauty. There was a flame in Fenella, an iron will, a spirit which had never been in her mother, and that love of adventure which had, perhaps, led her father to seek his fortune and make his way in the wilds of Canada. Mrs. Shaw had always complained of Fenella's determination which, when she was a small child, had shown itself. They had often clashed. A queer, rebellious little thing Fenella had been, never really understood by her mother. There was still something of the rebel in the straight glance of fearless eyes, the strong moulding of her wide mouth, and the doggedness of a young pointed chin.

Being left alone in the world had no terrors for Fenella. But once she landed in Canada, she grew conscious of acute homesickness and the sudden wish to be back in London with the mother whose love was at worst the only one Fenella had ever known. After all, she was only just twenty-one, and what did she know about life in Canada on a cattle ranch and this father whom she could not even remember? She was homesick and a little afraid when she arrived at Edmonton. And still more afraid when her father's manager met her, only to tell her that she would never know that father, and that he must for ever remain to her a stranger and a name. Dick Shaw had been killed in an accident, hunting beaver up the Hudson, a day before Fenella landed, and his funeral was Fenella's only welcome from him.

She was terribly lonely for weeks after that. Financially she found herself well off. Everything had been left to her. She was not unlucky to become the owner of a handsome bungalow and a flourishing ranch. But there seemed little suitable companionship for one of her years and upbringing. Except for the Indian women who were servants, there was nobody within miles. And then only the rough-and-ready Canadian wives of neighbouring ranchers.

Of necessity, she was thrown more than a little upon the company of her father's manager, Max Geering. Of German and English origin, Geering was a big, fair, handsome man of a powerful, athletic build, with sleepy, long-lidded eyes, and a Teutonic passion for music, outside his work. Fenella's father appeared to have placed infinite trust in him, and he seemed, indeed, a capable and efficient manager. Fenella was told all round that she could leave her business in his hands with utmost confidence. She also heard that Max had an eye for female beauty, and was something of a heart-breaker in the district. Such a reputation would arouse any woman's interest, and it was not long before the girl, Fenella, looked at and spoke to her manager with feminine curiosity as well as business instinct.

Max could be charming. Max made himself more than charming to his employer's daughter, now mistress of the Bar-None Ranch. Not only was she lovely, but she was lonely, and his own bungalow was but half a mile across the grazing-fields. He could come up in the long winter evenings, and play to her on the tinny old piano, from which his fingers managed to extract the utmost possible harmony. And he could sing, too. Little heart-breaking songs by Schumann and Schubert. In German, very appealingly, Max delivered these ballads.

There was nobody to advise Fenella. Nobody but the big blond Max to amuse her and drive away the depression of that first interminable winter when the snow seemed to fall without ceasing, and one couldn't get outside the door for days on end and the nights were cold, dark and terrifying; long silences broken only by the hungry cry of wolves from the surrounding forests.

Fenella had ample protection in her Indian servants. Tomasso, the Chippewayan who had been Mr. Shaw's devoted servant, would have died for 'Little White Lady,' as he called Fenella. And there were others ready to die for her. She had gained an immense popularity on the ranch. She had shown such spirit in learning to ride a horse, to shoot, to fish, and to endure physical hardship stoically like other women in the vicinity.

But it was not enough for her to have faithful followers or devoted slaves. Her heart, lonely and hungry as any girl's for human affection, cried for something more. And that something was supplied by Max.

Then in the New Year down at the saloon there had been a dance. Fenella in a pretty evening dress brought out from London, and Max, one of the only men to possess a dinner jacket, danced together the whole evening and made a handsome, devoted enough couple to cause all the tongues for miles round to wag freely for days afterwards. So it was not a matter for amazement when, at the end of January, it was announced that Fenella and Max were getting married.

Now the great day had come. Tomorrow was Max's and Fenella's wedding day. After tomorrow, Max would not need to come up here just to look through the accounts and talk business. He would move from his bungalow to hers, and stay here with her always. They would never be parted again. It was a delirious thought to Fenella, because she was very much in love with Max. And it was the first time in her life she had been in love and had known the intoxication of being adored in return.

There wasn't another man in the world like Max. So fair, so handsome, so clever. A man of education and culture, as well as one who could manage a cattle ranch and make money for her as he was doing. They would run the ranch together now. She would never sell it, as once she had thought of doing. Neither would she go back to England unless it was with Max, to introduce him to a few distant cousins, and friends at home.

Her heart was here now. Her life and love were here in this grand open country with its rolling, fertile plains and blue mountains, its great broad, shining rivers, and the fine spruce forests which lay so black and dense and mysterious under the big clear stars.

Tenderly and passionately, Fenella thought of her lover and of tomorrow. It would not be the sort of wedding which poor Mum would have liked, she reflected; in a nice conventional church, wearing a nice conventional wedding dress with veil and orange blossoms, and the rest of it. No smart crowd would gather at a reception to see her cut the cake. There would be no going away or honeymoon in the accepted sense of the word. She and Max had decided that they would wait until the summer, and then take a few weeks up in the mountains. But just now with the advancing of spring, and all the new cattle being born, it was advisable for Max to stay and superintend. They were to have the ceremony in the tiny chapel down the hill. Old Parson Jenkins came up from Edmonton on his sledge, driven by a pack of dogs, to perform Sunday service there when the weather permitted. Only a few people would be present. The boys on the ranch and some of the neighbours and traders. No 'reception'. Just a few drinks, then she and Max would steal up here to her bungalow, and here they would start the glory of their new existence together.

Tonight, a little wistfully, Fenella thought of the dead father she had never known, and wondered what he would have thought of her marriage to his manager. Wondered what he had really thought of Max as a man. Would he have liked to see his daughter become Mrs. Geering? Certainly her mother wouldn't have liked it. She had always wanted Fenella to marry well, and she would not have considered the manager of a cattle ranch a suitable husband. But Fenella thought him suitable. Fenella was only happy now when she was with Max. What a lover he was! Skilful enough, in fact, to make her wonder just how many other women he had held in his arms. He had had 'affairs', but he said that he had never really loved any girl but his Fenella.

This afternoon when she had seen him, and they had made the final arrangements for their marriage, he had kissed her mouth and her throat in that way which set her heart beating so madly, and he had whispered:

'One more night . . . and you'll belong to me. What heaven, my *liebling*, for us both.'

She loved that German word of

endearment which he used for her. She loved the way his sleepy blue eyes half closed when he looked at her, and the caress of his music-making hands, which he had kept quite fine and sensitive in spite of all the rough work he did on the ranch.

She had wanted to see him this evening, but he had told her that he would not come up to the bungalow tonight. He wished to make all the books up to date and leave everything in apple-pie order for the assistant manager to take over, in order that they might have a week of peace from tomorrow, and not allow the affairs of the ranch to trouble them any more than was necessary.

Fenella, wrapped from head to foot in soft brown beaver furs, roused herself from dreaming and, putting two slender fingers in her mouth, whistled like a boy for Tomasso to come with her sledge and her fine team of Eskimo dogs which Max had collected for her last winter. They were swift-running little dogs, and when the snow and ice were on the ground the Indian method of travelling was the surest and speediest. But after the big thaw, when the roads were dry, there was an old Ford motor-car which could take Fenella into the towns when she wanted to go.

Tomasso came round with the sledge, and Talooka, Fenella's Indian maid, came out to wrap her young mistress in fur rugs, for the March nights were freezing cold. Fenella smiled at Talooka. A lovely Indian child of seventeen, slim as a reed, with a skin like polished bronze, and glossy plaits, black as a raven's wing, swinging to her knees.

'Good night, Talooka, and don't wait up for me,' said Fenella.

The Indian girl kissed Fenella's hand and withdrew into the bungalow in silence. Fenella looked at the young Indian holding the dogs in check. He had an unusually sullen expression. He was Talooka's lover. Fenella had an idea that they had quarrelled. But they would make it up again now that the spring was coming, Fenella smiled to herself. Lovers could not be cross with each other for long in this intoxicating Canadian spring, which was meant for love and for happiness.

Fenella snuggled under her furs, closed her eyes and thought about Max, while the Indian let the dogs go, and they slid swiftly over the icy roads down to the saloon bar. Fenella had promised to put in an appearance this evening. There were a lot of the boys waiting to give her a toast and wish her luck for tomorrow.

She walked through the swing doors into the saloon, leaving the icy crisp atmosphere of the night for that hot, smoke laden room with some regret. But she felt very kindly disposed towards all the boys, and her grey eyes smiled at them as she entered. They were a grand lot, she thought. Big, honest-to-God ranchers and farmers, a great many of them in her employ. All of them had known and respected her father. A cheer went up as she entered.

'Here's Miss Fenella. 'Evening, Miss

Fenella, and good luck to you!'

Soon Fenella was seated on a stool, taking off her coat and mittens and cap. The flickering lights of the kerosene lamps gleamed on her short fair curls.

A variety of men crowded around her. Fur traders, mounted police, half-breeds, neighbouring ranchers. Drinks were flowing. Fenella sipped a glass of hot spiced wine because it was expected of her. A cowboy sat at the piano and beat out tunes which made Fenella wish that Max was here to give them some real music. There was a lot of talk and laughter and discussion of the coming wedding. One big Canadian, Tom Pincher, who worked on the Bar-None Ranch, threaded his way through the crowd, followed by a buxom, brown-haired young woman who was his wife. He lifted a glass of ale to Fenella.

'Good luck for tomorrow, Miss Fenella.'

Fenella, pink and radiant, smiled at him.

'Thanks, Tom. Thanks awfully.'

'You've sure got a good-looking bride-groom, Fenella,' said Meg Pincher.

'Yes,' said Fenella softly, 'Max *is* good looking.'

' 'Tain't looks that counts,' came from the high-pitched voice of an old man with a goatee beard behind them.

Fenella turned to the owner of the voice.

'You're right, Grandpa Jo, and it isn't only good looks that Max has. He's the best man in the world.'

'He sure knows how to shoot straight,' said Tom Pincher.

'And as long as a chap can shoot that's all that Tom thinks necessary,' put in Meg.

Fenella laughed at them.

'There *are* other things, eh, Meg?'

Meg Pincher nodded. She was a good-hearted woman, and very fond of Fenella. When Fenella had first come out from England, Meg, like many other of the ranchers' wives, had anticipated that the young Londoner might be too stuck-up and fine to make friends with them. But they had soon found that Fenella was not only strikingly lovely, but full of friendliness towards them all, and Meg was now one of her greatest admirers. Meg admired Max Geering too. There were few women out here who didn't. But there were one or two things she had heard about Max, one or two unpleasant little rumours which had come to her ears which left her a bit anxious on Fenella's behalf. Fenella wasn't like the rest of the girls, she thought, husky, Canadian-born, fit to meet trouble when it came in these wild parts. She was a spirited girl, but she was soft and inexperienced, and had been brought up in a different country. Meg hoped that nothing that Max would do or had done would ever break the bubble of Fenella's sweet illusions about him. And maybe Max meant to settle down now and be a good boy. It was time. He was nearing thirty, and he'd had his day with the women. Added to which he'd be a fool to do anything but settle down with a rare girl like Fenella Shaw. He was doing pretty well for himself, marrying a great beauty, who was also the mistress of the Bar-None Ranch.

'Is Max coming down tonight?' asked Meg, seating herself by her friend's side.

'No. He's going to work late on the books. But on the way back I may call in and pay him a surprise visit,' said Fenella.

'That ain't right,' said Meg. 'You shouldn't see your future husband the night before your marriage. It's unlucky.'

Fenella laughed.

'I'm not superstitious! And think of the poor darling huddled over those wretched accounts. I'm going to make him stop work and give him the thrill of seeing me.'

'Maybe he won't let you go if he gets you there.'

Fenella laughed, and the colour in her cheeks deepened.

'What rubbish! Oh course he will. He's not like that, Meg.'

'He's crazy about you, isn't he?'

'Yes, and so am I about him, but well . . . tomorrow will soon be here.'

'You believe in him absolutely, don't you, Fenella?'

Fenella gave her a surprised look.

'Yes. Why not?'

Meg made no answer.

'Don't you believe in your Tom?' added Fenella.

'Oh yes,' said Meg, slightly confused. But mentally she was of the opinion that the handsome Max, with his conceit of himself and his musical ability, so rare in a man out here, could hardly be compared with her dear old Tom, who was just a big lumbering fellow with a big capacity for rounding up cattle and drinking beer. Not that she wouldn't rather have Tom than Max if it came to that. She trusted Tom all right.

'What's in your mind, Meg?' asked Fenella.

'Oh, nothin', my dear.'

'Don't you believe in Max?'

Meg's honest face coloured.

'Now come,' said Fenella, 'I know

what's the matter. You've heard that Max has had affairs before he became engaged to me, and I know it. He doesn't deny it.'

'And you don't mind?'

'No, I don't mind what's happened before he and I became engaged I don't think any woman has a right to criticise a man for what he's done before he's hers. It's afterwards that counts.'

'You mean you wouldn't forgive anything he did now?'

Fenella's smoke-grey eyes grew suddenly cold and hard under their dense black lashes.

'Why should I? That's different. No girl would forgive a man being loose with other women *after* he'd pledged himself to her. But why are you talking like this, Meg? What are you insinuating?'

'Now, honey, don't be cross. I didn't mean anything at all,' said the good-hearted Meg, with much embarrassment. 'We was only talking, wasn't we?'

Fenella's face cleared and her eyes grew soft again.

'I trust Max just as much as he trusts me,' she said.

'Sure, honey.'

'And you can take it from me,' added Fenella with a flash of Irish spirit, 'that if any man played a dirty trick on me, I'd get back on him.'

'In what way?' asked Meg curiously.

'Goodness knows. But if I was betrayed or insulted I'd certainly do something desperate. I wouldn't sit back and weep.'

'You're a great kid,' said Meg.

A few moments later Fenella was laughing and joking with the boys. She was at the top of her form, and they howled with appreciation of her jests. She was happy. Yet at the back of her brain were restless little thoughts . . . little worrying remembrances of things that Meg Pincher had said. Why all that talk about Max and affairs and insinuations? Had Meg heard anything? . . . But no, Fenella was sure of her lover, and felt that she would be disloyal to harbour one little suspicion. They were to be married tomorrow. He would be hers and she would be his — for ever.

She had a sudden longing to see him. She wanted the reassurance of his arms. He was so big and strong, her Max. Her head barely touched his shoulder, and he would often pick her up as though she was a child and carry her round the room. Her feet, he said, were just the length of his hand, so small they were. She was his little lovely flower . . . his *liebling*. He would sit down at the piano and play and sing '*Ich liebe dich*' for her in his haunting voice.

She did not care about superstition. She was going to see her bridegroom tonight, even although they had arranged not to meet until tomorrow.

She put on her fur coat and cap and drew on her mittens. The boys gave her a final toast.

'Happiness for tomorrow, Miss Fenella.'

'Three cheers for our Lady of Bar-None Ranch.'

'To Miss Fenella and Mr. Max . . . '

She got away from them at last, her cheeks crimson and her eyes shining. Tomasso was there outside with the dogs snapping and snarling round the sledge. She told him to drive to Mr. Max's bungalow.

They went down the hill, slipping away from the saloon, the tinkle of the piano following them.

The crisp night was full of sounds. Fenella could hear the rushing torrents of melting snows and the chinking of ice as it cracked. The air seemed full of the sweetness of spruce saplings bursting into bud.

More than anything in the world, Fenella wanted Max, and the touch of his hands and his lips. It was an almost unbearable longing for him which she knew could not be assuaged until she was in his arms again. Tomorrow this fever would abate a little, perhaps. Tomorrow when she would be with him. And he felt like this for her. He had told her so a thousand times. How pleased and excited he would be to catch this unexpected glimpse of her tonight. She laughed softly at the thought of standing in the circle of his arms, while they exchanged good wishes for tomorrow.

Only a few hours more now before that Tomorrow, the glory of morning, the spring sunshine melting more ice and snow, unfolding the blossom, and bringing the birds and animals out into the open. For now the great grand courtship of all living things was beginning.

The sledge drew up before Max Geering's small bungalow. It was a much less luxurious and pretentious affair than the one which Fenella's father had built for himself on top of the hill. Fenella looked round and could see no lights. For a moment she wondered if she had come too late, and that Max had grown tired of work and had gone to bed.

But she felt that she must see him . . . if only for an instant. Tomasso pulled the fur rugs from her knees. She got up and ran on to the porch and softly pushed open the door of the bungalow.

2

Max Geering's living-room was in darkness and shadows save for the red embers of the dying log fire. Fenella stood still a moment, her eyes full of eager anticipation. She called:

'Max! Max!'

No answer. Fenella called again. Was Max out? Or was he so sound asleep that he did not even hear her voice? She drew off her mittens, fumbled in her pocket with cold little fingers and found a box of matches. Striking one, she looked around. She had not often been to Max's place. Generally he came up to her. But she knew this room pretty well. The rosewood German piano, which was a better one than her father's and which was going to be moved up to her bungalow tomorrow. The couch with white bearskin rugs thrown over it. The striped curtains, and walls covered with Indian weapons, skins, beaded ornaments. More primitive than the home which Fenella's father had made for himself and furnished in a civilised style.

The match went out. Fenella struck another. It seemed to her that Max could only have just left the room, for there was a cigarette-end burning in an ashtray beside the couch. He might have just gone into his bedroom. She called to him again. But there was silence.

A trifle uneasily Fenella applied her match to the kerosene lamp which stood on the table. She thought she heard a voice and a scuffle behind that door which communicated with Max's bedroom. And suddenly a feeling of strange uneasiness came across her. She walked to the door and opened it. Her astonished gaze fell upon the figure of her lover standing there in the lamplit bedroom. Max, in a state of half dress, velveteen trousers, red flannel check shirt, open at the neck, his yellow hair ruffled. He looked as though he had just got out of bed. His face was not like the face of the Max she knew. It was livid and furious. She was struck dumb by the fury on it. Her eyes travelled speedily to a far corner of the room, and came to rest on the familiar figure of a slim Indian girl wearing the traditional fringed tunic and trousers of soft leather, embroidered with beads. *Talooka*. Fenella's half-breed Indian maid, crouching there with a look of fear and guilt on her brown, pretty face.

For an instant Fenella stood turned to stone, her brain almost paralysed, conscious of nothing but horrified amazement. Then with a little cry she turned and walked back into the sitting-room. Immediately Max Geering sprang after her.

'Fenella! Don't go. Fenella, I . . . '

'Don't speak to me!' she broke in, and swung round to face him, white and trembling. 'Don't ever speak to me again.'

'*Ach Gott*, Fenella, wait a minute and let me explain.'

'You couldn't explain. My maid. My Indian servant. And tomorrow ... ' Her voice cracked. ' . . . Tomorrow we were going to get married.'

'But we still are,' he said in a panic-stricken voice. 'Fenella, *liebling,* you're putting a wrong construction on this. I tell you I can explain.'

Her small fists doubled in the pockets of her fur coat. Her grey eyes blazed up into his face. A face scarlet with discomfiture now, and, to her distorted imagination, with guilt written all over it. She panted:

'You said you wouldn't come and see me because you had work to do. But you asked my maid up to amuse you. A charming pastime. And I came to give you a surprise. Oh, God!'

She broke down completely and turned to flee. Max Geering barred her way through the door by standing against it. From his great height he looked down at her, pleadingly.

'Listen, *liebling,* I tell you you're making a mistake. *Ach,* if you'll only listen to me, I'll explain.'

'You can't. Talooka is here in your bedroom and you've spent the evening with her.'

'Fenella . . . '

'I don't want to see you again!' she cut in passionately, 'I'd rather marry anybody but you. You've always had a bad reputation with women, but I didn't believe it. Even Meg said something funny about you tonight, but I wouldn't listen to her. Thank God I did come along. Thank God I found you out before I married you.'

'Don't be a little fool,' he said more roughly. 'You know perfectly well that I only love you and will never love anybody but you.'

She tore off her ring, the solitaire diamond which Max had bought her in Edmonton to celebrate their engagement. She tossed it on the table.

'I've finished with you. Let me go.'

Then he gave a little laugh and caught her in his arms. She looked so lovely in her rage and he exulted in her jealousy. He knew the potency of his love-making. If he could not make her listen to his words, he could at least make her *feel*. He caught her close and brushed her eyelids and her cheeks with his lips, kissed the protests from her mouth. For a moment she could not think straight. Max's kisses had always set her heart spinning at a mad rate. But when she did remember that Indian girl in the other room . . . Max had been kissing her, too . . . reason returned to Fenella and she pushed him away.

'Let me pass,' she sobbed, and tore out of the bungalow into the frosty, sparkling night.

He followed her out on to the porch, calling after her.

'Come back, Fenella. Crazy one, come back. I can explain if you'll only let me. Fenella . . . I love you! Fenella, we're going to be married tomorrow . . . '

But she took no notice, and ran like one pursued over the snow and reached the sledge. Sobbing and gasping, she

31

jumped in, drew the fur robes over her and bade Tomasso take her home.

She sat back with a hand across her eyes, labouring under the most frightful and passionate jealousy. With all her heart and soul she had loved Max. It was vile — horrible — to have found Talooka, her own Indian maid, there with him tonight. She had believed in him implicitly. And so lightly did he hold her that he had had to be amused by an Indian servant the very night before his marriage. He was a brute and a beast. A handsome, cruel beast. But she had adored him, and tomorrow she was to have become his wife. How was she going to endure it?

Never had she suffered so much as in this moment while the sledge took her over the freezing road up to her bungalow. It would not have been so bad if the thing that she had found out had killed her love for Max. But it hadn't. She was just wildly jealous of Talooka, and she still wanted Max. She had known when he touched her lips with his just now that he still had the power to thrill her. If she had stayed with him a moment longer, her passion for him would have weakened her to such an extent that she might have forgiven him.

She must never forgive, she told herself. All her Irish pride was in revolt. Pride and love together rebelling fiercely against Max's infidelity on the very eve of their wedding. She thought:

'I wish I could kill him. I wish I could punish them both.'

And she felt that if there had been another man — another suitor for her hand — she would have married him this very night out of sheer primitive rage.

The sledge pulled up before her bungalow. Tomasso helped her out. She looked at the boy's impassive brown face and remembered that he was Talooka's lover. Poor Tomasso! How would he feel about it if he knew that his woman was down there in that bungalow with the white man? Talooka was without shame, and so was Max. Oh, but she could kill them both!

She sent Tomasso away and walked unsteadily across the porch to her front door. It was as though a film dimmed her eyes and she could not see properly. She shook with the violence of her emotions.

As she put her hand on the door knob, a silhouette fell across the moon-light. She turned with a startled cry to see a man standing behind her. He must have just come out of the shadows at the far end of the porch.

'Who is it?' she gasped. 'Who are you?'

For a moment the stranger did not speak. Fenella stared at him. He was a tall man, although not as tall or as broad as Max. She had never seen him before in her life. He did not belong in these parts. The moon revealed him as a man of slim and graceful build, dressed in very British clothes, a brown tweed coat, riding breeches and gaiters. He had a woollen muffler round his neck. He wore no hat. She could see that his hair was black, but that he had a strange white lock sweeping straight back from his forehead. He looked thin, hard as nails, brown-skinned, and had eyes of a light shade of blue. Altogether an unusual-looking man, attractive rather than handsome. He seemed somewhat dishevelled and his clothes were thickly powdered with snow.

'Who on earth are you?' demanded Fenella.

'That doesn't matter,' he said.

He spoke in a low voice. A cultured English voice, which surprised her still more.

'What do you want?' she asked.

'A horse.'

'Why should you come to me for a horse?'

'Because this is the first dwelling I've hit upon in miles. I'm on my way up the valley. I've got to reach Troit Pass tonight. My own mount has just thrown me and broken its leg. I had to shoot the poor beast.'

A voice with a faint trace of an Irish brogue. Fenella, in spite of her own distracted condition of mind, could not fail to be intrigued.

'Where have you come from?' she asked.

'That can't matter to you,' he said.

'You want me to lend you a horse, and are not even polite enough to tell me your name.'

'It can't matter to you,' he repeated.

'Do you know who I am?'

'No, and I shan't ask.'

She gave a short laugh.

'You're a queer man.'

'Will you lend me the horse?' he said impatiently.

'Perhaps.'

'I beg you to. It means more than I can ever tell you. Life or death, in fact.'

Still more intrigued, Fenella stared at the stranger. She could see that he was in a nervous condition and that he seemed out of breath, as though he had been running.

'Troit Pass is twenty miles from here,' she said. 'Are you going to try to make it tonight?'

'I've got to. If you don't let me have

the horse, I must walk.'

'In that case you'd be there by tomorrow night,' she said. 'And half frozen in those clothes.'

He put his cupped hands to his mouth and blew on them.

'I'm half frozen now,' he said grimly. 'That doesn't matter.'

'You'd better come in and have a spot of whisky.'

'I won't if you don't mind. Just tell me where your stables are.'

'You're very cool,' said Fenella.

'Look here, for God's sake do what I ask,' he said urgently.

She contemplated him a moment. After her scene with Max she felt crazy . . . ready to do anything. She felt raw and resentful and unlike herself. She wanted to do something mad . . . to pay Max back . . . to show him that she didn't care about Talooka . . . that he could do what he liked and she would do what she liked, too.

With that madness on her she gave way to the craziest impulse of her life.

She looked up into the light blue eyes of the strange Englishman with the white lock in the blackness of his hair.

'Are you English?' she asked him.

'Oh, God,' he said impatiently, 'what interest can that be to you?'

'Answer me.'

He shrugged his shoulders.

'Irish.'

She gave an excited laugh.

'I thought so. Your hair and your eyes and your voice. Ireland bred them. I'm half Irish, too. They can be a crazy lot. You're a bit crazy, aren't you? There's a mystery about you. Perhaps you've done something wrong. Perhaps you're escaping from the police ... *are you?*'

He did not change colour. Not a muscle in his face moved. He said:

'I'm answering no questions.'

'Well, I don't care who or what you are. You want a horse. I'll lend you the fastest in my stable if you'll ride with me first to the parson's house and marry me.'

Silence. The stranger looked thunder-struck. With newly awakened interest he looked down at the girl. He saw that she was young and dressed richly in the finest beaver skins, and that under the little fur cap was a very beautiful face. Grey eyes 'put in with a smutty finger' . . . eyes that he knew came from the Ireland which had been his home in his boyhood. He and this girl had something kindred in their blood which he recognised, as she had done. And he knew of this wildness in the blood, and this madness which could possess the people of their country. But this was a little too mad even for him.

'Girl, are you a lunatic?' he asked.

'Perhaps,' said Fenella.

'You want me to marry you?'

'Yes.'

'In return for a loan of a horse?'

'I'll give it to you.'

'Handsome,' he said with a laugh, and folded his arms, 'but not a fair exchange. My name and my freedom in return for a mount.'

'You're free to do what you like, aren't you?'

'Quite,' he said. 'I've done plenty of things, but I've never got myself involved with a woman yet.'

'You needn't see me again after tonight,' she said.

His lashes, as black and thick as hers, flickered.

'Might I ask what the marriage is for?'

'Yes,' said Fenella. 'Tomorrow I was to be married to the manager of my ranch. I found out that he's got my Indian girl in his bungalow. The parson who was to have married us is down in the shack beside the chapel. If you'll come with me and go through the form of marriage, I'll pay you anything you like.'

He stared at her curiously. It was a hair-brained scheme. A matter of revenge. The beautiful, fair-haired girl was mad with pique and jealousy, and she wanted to pay back her faithless lover.

'How will it help you tying yourself up to me?' he asked.

The moonlight showed her young face drained of colour, and her eyes large and wounded.

'I'd like to face him tomorrow and tell him that I've married someone else. I'm afraid of him, and still more afraid of myself, and I want to make it impossible for me to marry him — or forgive him. I've finished with love for ever.'

The stranger hesitated. She was mad, indeed. But so was he tonight, and *he must have that horse.*

'Are you quite sure that you want to do it?' he asked.

'Quite sure.'

'And we're never to see each other again after the ceremony?'

'Never.'

'How do you know I won't come back and make demands on you?'

She looked him straight in the eyes.

'I don't think you will. You've got your own life to lead, and it has nothing to do with mine.'

'You're right, my child. Very well. If

41

those are your terms, I'll take them. But let's get on with it. I've got to get to Troit Pass, and the sooner the better.'

'Will you follow me, please?' said Fenella.

He walked with her to the stables. Tomasso had put away the dogs and gone. Fenella found a stable lamp, and the stranger lit it. In silence she took her own favourite hunter, and then chose a big grey mare for him. Max usually rode that mare. The more she thought of Max, the more she hated the thought of him and that Indian girl up there. And the stronger grew her madness for this revenge. She was going to ruin her life. But Max had already ruined it. She was finished with love, as she had just told this Irishman. It didn't matter what she did. And there was something strangely satisfying about this crazy action which she was about to commit.

In silence they saddled the two horses, and the next moment they were galloping over the snow and down the hill to the parson's shack. As they rode, Fenella stole a glance at the stranger and thought how well he rode that mare. Better than Max. He rode almost like an Indian, with the same virile grace. Max was inclined to pull at the animal's mouth, and the mare was never very easy under him. But she went like a bird with the stranger on her back.

'I think,' said Fenella, as they dismounted in front of the parson's shack beside the chapel, 'that I'd better know your name.'

He laughed grimly.

'Just as well, since it's to be yours. I'm Gail O'Shean.'

'O'Shean,' repeated Fenella. 'Then you're from the west coast?'

'Yes.'

'So was my mother. And my name is Fenella Shaw.'

He gave her a quick look.

'Fenella O'Shean goes uncommonly well,' he said softly.

They knocked up the parson. The old man came down with a coat over his night attire, a little scared by this nocturnal visit. But when he saw Fenella he was relieved. The relief changed to astonishment when she told him what she wished him to do. He had come here to marry the lady of Bar-None Ranch to Max Geering. What in heaven's name possessed her to bring this stranger down to him at midnight and tie herself up to him?

Fenella stopped all questioning. She was determined that the marriage should take place, and the old clergyman felt better at the sight of the money that she produced. Times were hard in this outlandish spot, and there was not much of a living for him. He would have married anybody for a few pounds. He called the old half-breed woman who cooked for him, as a witness.

There in the sparsely furnished room of the wooden shack, by the light of two candles, and with a cold northern wind whistling through the draughty window panes, Fenella and the stranger were made man and wife.

It was only when the actual ceremony was finished, and Fenella wrote her maiden name for the last time in the book beside that of Gail O'Shean, that she realised to the full the madness of what she had done. Well . . . it was too late to retract now. And it would be something to tell Max when he came for her in the morning.

She found herself shivering with cold. Gail O'Shean had tossed down a drink that the parson had offered him. Wiping his lips, he turned to her.

'Do you mind if I go now?' he said.

She looked at him speechlessly. On her finger was an old gold ring which had belonged to her mother. She had brought it for the ceremony. Gail O'Shean had just put it on her finger. She felt that she had no strength left . . . not even the strength to take that ring off again.

'Yes, go if you like.'

'Would you rather I took you home first?'

'I'm used to riding alone. If you want

to get to Troit Pass, you'd better be starting.'

He came nearer her. For the first time something of sympathy showed in his face, relaxing the granite. They looked at each other as though they were human beings.

'You've done a mad thing tonight,' he said.

'I realise that. But what's it matter?'

'You're very trusting. I might come back.'

'But you won't, will you?'

A shadow — was it of regret? — flickered in the man's light blue eyes. He looked down at the lovely sensitive face of the girl. His wife. Beautiful, and from his own country. And he was never to see her again. Well, he had promised her, and it was a promise he would keep.

'No, I won't,' he said. 'You've nothing to fear from me.'

She shivered. How cold she was! How tired! All passions, love, hatred, revenge, all were dying down to a feeling of stony misery and of some dismay at the thing

46

she had just done.

'Then goodbye,' she said.

He took her hand and raised it to his lips with an old-world courtesy.

'Goodbye, and good luck, Fenella O'Shean.'

There was a tinge of amusement in his voice, and suddenly he smiled, and she was disconcerted to find that he was charming.

And after that he was gone. He walked out of the parson's shack and rode away on his horse into the night. She could hear the crunch of the horse's hooves on the soft snow — then silence.

Like one in a dream, Fenella paid the parson and bade him goodbye, mounted her own chestnut and turned up the hill again towards her bungalow.

She was like a dazed person. She could only think confusedly. But all thoughts culminated into the memory of Gail O'Shean's smile and of his haunting voice saying:

'Goodbye, and good luck, Fenella O'Shean.'

That was her new name. And the marriage contract was in her pocket and the ring on her finger.

Then she thought of Max and tomorrow, which was to have been her wedding-day.

'God in heaven, what have I done?' she asked herself. All that was frozen in her came to life. She galloped back to her bungalow furiously, riding the chestnut like one possessed with fear.

3

Fenella found it difficult to sleep. Her dreams were haunted by the stranger, Gail O'Shean, whom she had married. And the wedding-ring on her marriage finger burned her flesh like fire.

She was up and dressed early that morning. It was a stormy day — this day which should have marked Fenella's marriage to her manager. A grey, sullen-skied morning. The air was chill and black storm clouds hung low over the mountains. Down the gloomy river, sullen and dark, great cakes of ice were float-ing, and the hunger cry of wolves echoed from the spruce forests beyond.

Fenella, warmly clad in a skirt made of soft red suède, a red leather coat, and a white wool jersey with a polo collar up to her chin, stared out of the window at the figures of the cowboys moving about the ranch. She felt sick with misery and nerves. She had dressed herself this morning without Talooka's help. She was glad she had not set eyes on Talooka. But as she stood here in the sitting-room, the slender figure of the Indian girl, in her fringed dress, moved softly on her moccasins across to her Lady. Immediately all Fenella's bitter jealousy and resentment of last night returned. She looked at Talooka in anger and bitterness. But Talooka, with soft, pleading liquid eyes, smiled back at her.

'Mistress,' she said, 'Talooka wishes to leave her Lady.'

'That is expected,' said Fenella coldly.

'Talooka is getting married tomorrow.'

Fenella stiffened in every limb.

'And to whom?'

'To Tomasso, Mistress.'

The blood rushed to Fenella's cheeks. She stared at the Indian girl.

'And does Tomasso know about last night?' she asked, her hands clenched behind her back.

The Indian girl gave her mistress a timid, appealing look.

'All can be explained, Mistress. Me love nobody but Tomasso. Me always love him, but we quarrel over moose-skin he promise me. Tomasso, he always do what Mr. Geering say on ranch, and so I go up to Mr. Geering last night. Ask him to put quarrel right. He promise, and then come knock at door and you there. No understand. Me think it Tomasso and might kill me if find me in Mr. Geering's bungalow, so hide in bedroom. You no listen for Mr. Geering, and so now he veree, veree sad. But Mr. Geering love his White Lady, and she make one big mistake.'

The words poured out in Talooka's clipped, funny little voice. Fenella looked into the big black eyes and saw nothing but truth in them. She hardly knew what she felt. But mainly she felt overwhelming remorse. Talooka loved Tomasso, and they were to be married tomorrow. Talooka had gone up to

Max's bungalow to plead with him to reunite her with her Indian lover. There had been no foundation for all her jealousies and suspicions. And she had refused to let Max explain. Something seemed to grip her by the throat.

'Oh, God!' she thought, 'what have I done?'

The door of the living-room was pushed open. A big, yellow-haired man, wearing riding clothes and carrying a crop, walked in. Fenella gave one anguished look at Max's face, that handsome face, that handsome blond head. He stood still and looked back at her with an expression of deep reproach.

'Well?' he said.

Talooka glided from the room. Just as she reached the door she passed Max and gave him a swift, upward glance, which was both significant and satisfied. The door closed behind her, and Max went on looking at Fenella.

'Well?' he said again. 'Has Talooka explained, or do you want more explanations from me?'

Fenella could not reply. She felt choked. She was as white as the snows that lay outside in the fields. Her knees were trembling so that she had to sit down. In a bewildered way she ran her slim fingers through her crop of silvery fair curls and shook them helplessly, hopelessly.

'What have I done?' was all she could think or say.

Max came nearer her.

'I ought to be angry with you,' he said. 'I ought to be furious and indignant for what you thought of me. It was an insult. And yet I can't be angry. You were just jealous, weren't you, *liebling?* But you understand now, do you?'

She looked up, and there were two red spots on her cheek bones.

'Yes, I understand now.'

'Thank God for that,' was his inner reflection, but aloud he said in a rich, wounded voice:

'*Ach,* my Fenella, how could you have thought such a thing of me?'

Still no answer from her. And then he

53

went down on one knee beside her and, with the old intimate gesture, tilted back her head and kissed first her throat and then her lips. But those lips were dry and her cheeks were ashen. He drew back in amazement.

'You don't still suspect me? You know that I was only trying to help Talooka and Tomasso?'

'Yes.'

'You have nothing more to be jealous of?'

'No.'

'Then why don't you kiss me? *Liebling*, this is our wedding day. Fenella . . . '

'Don't,' she whispered. 'Don't kiss me. Oh, Max, what have I done?'

'What *have* you done?' he asked uneasily.

She shook from head to foot.

'I — can't marry you now.'

'Why not?'

'Max, last night I believed that you and Talooka . . . Oh, God, I didn't realise she had gone to you about Tomasso.' She drew a slip of paper from her pocket and showed it to him. 'I did *this*.'

Geering stared at it. He saw that it was a certificate of marriage . . . signed by Fenella Shaw and Gail O'Shean.

'You see . . . it's too late,' she said. 'I — am married — to this man.'

Max's fair, ruddy face became convulsed. A mist came over his eyes. A mist of rage. He felt sick with fury and disappointment. The little fool . . . to have done such a mad thing. She was mistress of Bar-None Ranch and rich — and he, Max Geering, had wanted her and her possessions more than anything in the world.

Fenella burst into tears.

'Forgive me, Max — forgive me. I didn't know. I thought you and Talooka were lovers . . . I went off my head!'

He sank into a chair and bowed his head between his hands.

'This is a terrible blow — *ach Gott*. It will kill me,' he said, 'and ruin you.'

Fenella flung herself on her knees beside him. She put her arms around him.

'Max, darling — it was my mad jealousy. I thought you really had played the fool with Talooka. It made me wild. Oh, Max, this is awful. What can I do? What can we do?'

He lifted her from her knees and drew her on to his lap. He made mad love to her, drank her tears with passionate kisses, called her by every endearing name he could conjure up. Never had he been such a lover. Fenella was overcome with remorse, lay mute in his arms, bitterly reproaching herself for having wronged him. Mad, mad and foolish to have shown such a lack of faith!

At last Max spoke to her in a broken and sorrowful voice:

'Who is this Gail O'Shean you married, you mad little thing?'

'I — don't know.'

'A stranger.'

'Yes — I'd never seen him before. He was on my porch when I came home last night. He rode on to the Troit Pass. I don't know his business. I just lent him a horse.'

'You mean he stole it. Did you give him money?'

'A little — yes.'

'Oh, *liebling,* my crazy one.'

She put one of his hands against her cheek.

'Oh, Max,' she groaned, 'forgive me and tell me we can get this marriage annulled.'

'We can, and we will. I'll see the Sheriff at once. But first we must find him, whoever he is, this Gail O'Shean. An annulment is a mutual thing, and he must sign as well as you.'

'Are you sure it will be all right?' she asked feverishly.

Max stood up. He felt thwarted and enraged, but he managed to smile at her.

'I shall do it somehow, *liebling.* You don't imagine I shall wait a day longer for my wife than I have to.'

'I don't know why you're so forgiving — so kind. I wonder you don't want to kill me.'

'I only want to kill him,' said Max in a lordly way.

'He was desperate and didn't seem to care what happened to him. It was my fault really. In the clear light of day I begin to wonder how I could have been such a lunatic.'

Max took her hands and kissed them.

'*Ach Gott*,' he said ruefully, 'I didn't think you were such a mad little thing, Fenella.'

She clung to him. They exchanged frantic caresses. Never had he felt her more utterly his. Never had Fenella believed in Max more implicitly, nor been so ashamed of herself. When he left her to see the Sheriff she wept herself sick and blind. On the way out, Max saw Talooka in the porch. He whispered as he passed her:

'I'll see you some time, pretty one. Go through with this marriage to Tomasso — otherwise *she*'ll suspect. Keep our secret and I'll send you money . . .'

Talooka grinned and nodded.

All that morning Fenella remained in her room and refused to see a soul. Word went round the ranch that Miss

Fenella was ill. The wedding was postponed. The old padre and his servant who had witnessed the marriage between Miss Fenella and the stranger were sworn to secrecy. The ranchers imagined Miss Fenella and Max would fix things up either later in the day or tomorrow.

But Fenella, refusing to be comforted, moped and fretted, regretting her madness of last night. She knew that it would be days before she could get that midnight marriage annulled, so that she could marry her Max. Max, whom she had wronged, and who had been marvellous enough to understand and forgive her.

A second and crushing blow descended on her that afternoon. The Sheriff of the County arrived. An important man whose duties were divided between Edmonton and the surrounding settlements. He brought with him a warrant for the arrest of a dangerous outlaw. Posters, with photographs of this man, were put in every dwelling and on every gate in the district.

Max, as manager of the Bar-None

Ranch, brought the Sheriff to see Miss Shaw. Fenella, looking pale and exhausted by grief, received him, offered him drinks, then questioned him about the criminal for whom the law was searching. But her mind wandered from that subject to the thought of Max.

'He's a very desperate outlaw, Missy,' said the Sheriff, 'wanted for the hold-up of many a horseman and car on the mountain passes. Sure, he's a cunning rogue. There hasn't been a man amongst us who can keep him in gaol. They call him '*Phantom Hoofs*' — because he is a wonderful rider, I will say. Well, he was arrested in Edmonton a few days ago, but he escaped us — there's no bar or lock as can hold 'Phantom Hoofs,' far as I can see. Here's his photo. Queer man, Missy . . . youngish . . . but with one snow-white lock of hair front of his head . . .'

'*What!*' came from Fenella.

The two men looked at her. She had sprung to her feet and was staring at the photograph on the poster the Sheriff held out to her. She felt sick as

she looked at it. One white lock of hair
. . . yes . . . and there was no mistaking
that thin, hard face with the piercing
eyes . . . 'Phantom Hoofs' and Gail
O'Shean were one and the same. The
man she had married last night was the
desperate outlaw for whom Alberta was
hunting. She might have guessed it
. . . when he had begged for a horse. He
had been fleeing from justice. She
recalled his splendid, graceful figure on
the grey mare. He was 'Phantom
Hoofs.' And she was his wife.

She looked at the wedding-ring still
on her finger. Then, with a little sob,
she crumpled up on the floor.

'Fenella, *liebling*!' cried Max, and
rushed to her.

She had fainted.

When she recovered consciousness,
the Sheriff had gone. She was alone
with Max. She lay on the sofa, clinging
to his hand with both hers, and told
him what she now knew.

'Do you see — how dreadful — how
ghastly it is, Max? I am Mrs. Gail

O'Shean — wife of 'Phantom Hoofs.' Until they capture him, I can never get free — never get my marriage annulled. Only by mutual consent can we get free.'

Max Geering swore under his breath. This was a more serious affair than he had at first thought. He tried to comfort and reassure Fenella. But he felt ugly and thwarted, and he would like to have snarled at her.

'It'll be all right, *liebling*,' he said. 'I'll fix it. You say this fellow made for the Troit Pass last night at eleven o'clock? On my grey mare. Good. I'll put the Sheriff on to that. We won't tell a soul that you married him. Not a soul. And listen, darling — who knows that in some desperate struggle, this wretched outlaw will be shot — killed. That will automatically set you free.'

Fenella lay rigid, staring before her. She seemed to see the slim, graceful figure of Gail O'Shean standing in this room . . . to see a pair of light Irish blue eyes, smiling at her out of a thin, brown face . . . to hear a low, musical voice say:

'Goodbye, and good luck, Fenella O'Shean.'

And that was 'Phantom Hoofs' — the most reckless outlaw in Canada. A cultured man. No rough criminal, as might have been imagined.

Max left her sobbing her heart out. He gave the Sheriff an account of the visit of a man with one snow-white lock of hair, who resembled the photograph of 'Phantom Hoofs,' and had borrowed a horse from Miss Fenella last night.

The Sheriff was interested, but not wildly so.

'It's too late,' he said gloomily, 'he'll have got many miles from Troit Pass by now. It's nearly a whole day since he was here. Pity we didn't know 'bout it before.'

Max went to Fenella's bungalow again after supper that night. He felt cheated . . . angry. This should have been his wedding-night. He cursed himself for his indiscretion of last night. Damn Fenella and her unexpected visit. She might never have known of his affair with Talooka, whom he had seduced before her seventeenth birthday, and who had been visiting him all through the winter while he wooed and won his former master's daughter and heiress. And damn Fenella for playing this trick on him — tying herself up to an utter stranger!

When he entered Fenella's sitting-room, his face bore no sign of anger or irritation. He looked pale and tired — with just an attractive touch of grief — of reproach in his eyes — reproach which Fenella felt she deserved.

'The whole country's out after this outlaw, dearest,' he said, 'and we can only hope he'll be found soon, and then we can get this unfortunate marriage annulled. Oh, Fenella — I can't endure to think that tonight, by rights, we should be alone . . . man and wife . . . my darling . . . '

She, too, was tired and pale and worn out with crying. He sat beside her on the sofa before a big log fire. It was quiet and warm in the sitting-room. Fenella was wearing one of her pretty velvet dinner-dresses which she had brought out from England, and in which Max's sensuous nature revelled. Black velvet with a little cape of soft fur. Pearl ear-rings and the wheaten-coloured hair curling to the nape of a white neck. She was lovely and desirable. And she was mistress of Bar-None Ranch. Never had Max Geering felt a keener passion for her than tonight . . . when he realised that she was married to another man.

With an angry gesture he threw the cigarette which he had been smoking into the log fire. Fenella was not looking at him. She was sitting with her hands clasped over her knees, staring into that fire. He said:

'It's not so good, realising that tonight was to have been *our* night, whereas now I've got to leave you.'

She turned to him, her face flushing slowly until it was one burning blush.

'Don't, Max,' she said, 'don't make me more ashamed of myself than I am already.'

He looked down at her left hand. The firelight caught the gleam of gold on her marriage finger.

'Must you wear that damn ring?' he asked roughly.

'No,' she said in a low voice. 'It is my mother's ring, but I won't wear it if you don't want me to.'

'I don't,' he said between his teeth, and pulled it off. She was silent after that. Queer, but it felt wrong for him to have taken off that ring, since Gail O'Shean had put it there and the parson had made them man and wife.

'It was no real marriage,' said Max, as though he had read her thoughts. 'You needn't feel yourself married to that criminal, Fenella.'

'It's strange,' she said in a low voice, 'but I would have staked my life that he was anything but a criminal. I thought he was running away from something, but I would never have thought he was an outlaw ... a man like 'Phantom Hoofs.''

'Well, he is, and perhaps it was one of

his little games — marrying himself to you.'

'That couldn't be. It was I who suggested the marriage.'

'*Ach Gott,* let's forget it or I shall go mad.'

She leaned towards him.

'Some men would have refused to speak to me again — wiped the floor with me for going out and doing what I did. But you're so wonderful.'

'Don't you realise that I love you?' he asked, and caught her in his arms.

'I'll never forgive myself, Max. How can I make it up to you?'

He held her close, maddened by the warmth of her and the faint elusive fragrance of lilies . . . the scent she used . . . he always connected lilies with Fenella. He began to make mad love to her. Only for a minute she surrendered, and then fought through her own rising feeling for him.

'Don't, Max . . . Max . . . you mustn't kiss me any more . . . dearest . . . *please*!'

He, intoxicated with the sweetness of her responsive lips, covered her with kisses, poured out his longing with frenzied words:

'Don't send me away, tonight . . . Fenella . . . *liebling* . . . don't send me away. I love you . . . I can't bear this . . . tonight you were to have belonged to me absolutely. Forget this crazy marriage . . . this damned outlaw . . . forget you ever doubted me and went through that mad ceremony. Let me hold you in my arms tonight . . . my darling, my little Fenella . . .'

'No, no, Max — you're mad — let me go . . .'

'*Ach Gott,* Fenella, please . . .'

'Max — don't kiss me again — you mustn't. You're sending me out of my mind . . .'

'I want you to forget everything . . . except that you love me and want me as much as I want you,' he said, and buried his flushed face against the cool silk of her hair.

Her pulses raced and thrilled. She felt almost faint in that mad embrace.

But she was alive to the danger of the moment; and knew that the most acute danger of all was her own weak wish to surrender to her lover. She, too, wanted to forget her mad marriage, to wake up from that nightmare and find herself Max's wife — which, by all rights, she should have been this night. But something held her back. Principles, conventions, the instinctive desire to do what was right. And for some queer reason, in the very midst of that tornado of feeling, she seemed to see a pair of light blue eyes, smiling down at her, charmingly. The figure of a man, straight as a die in the saddle . . . and a low voice calling her 'Fenella O'Shean.'

She was Gail O'Shean's wife. Wife of this outlaw known as 'Phantom Hoofs.' She could not forget that. She must not surrender to Max tonight — because of 'Phantom Hoofs.'

The next moment she had torn herself from Max's arms. White and trembling, she stood by the fire, the back of her hand pressed to her lips.

'Please, please go, Max,' she said.

He came up to her and would have caught her back in his arms, but she waved him away.

'No, Max — please go.'

'Then you don't love me, Fenella.'

'I love you — too much,' she said, 'that's why you must go.'

He bit hard on his lip. But he saw that if he stayed against her will, he would alienate her. He bowed his head.

'I'm your humble servant — always, my *liebling*.'

'Try to understand . . . please . . . '

'I do. But this night's tragedy is killing me.'

'It's killing me, too,' she whispered, and sank on to the sofa again, burying her face in her hands.

When she looked up — Max had gone. The fire was dying down. The wind howled round the bungalow. A sudden snow storm had broken out. The white flakes whirled and spat against the window-panes. And Fenella felt intolerable loneliness and grief.

She turned out the lamps and walked slowly into her bedroom. Talooka had lit a wood fire there. It was warm and welcoming. Her green velvet dressing-gown and a nightgown of delicate silk lace had been laid on the bed ready for her. One of the pretty silky things she had worked on during the long winter evenings for her trousseau. She undressed and slipped into bed, heavy-hearted and afraid. She hid her face in the pillow and whispered her lover's name:

'Max. Max!'

She knew that the strongest thing she had ever done in her life was sending him away from her tonight.

She blew out the lamp by her bed-side. The room was plunged in darkness save for the comforting glimmer of the dying fire. Presently she dozed.

Later she woke up with a violent start and sat bolt upright in bed — wide-eyed — her heart pounding. She could hear the unmistakable sound of her window being opened. Too frightened to move or light a lamp, or call for

Talooka, Fenella sat there, dumb, staring at the window. She saw it moving upwards. The blue-and-white curtains bulged out as a figure climbed over the sill.

'Oh, God — who is it?' she thought.

There was just sufficient firelight for her to make out the shape of a tall, slimly built man. Then the curtains parted, and the intruder stood before her.

'Who are you?' she gasped.

The figure bowed. A low, mocking voice answered:

'*Your husband!*'

A match was struck. By the tiny light of that flame Fenella saw a thin brown face and a black head with one white, outstanding lock of hair. And she knew that this was Gail O'Shean — the man she had married last night. The man whom Alberta knew as 'Phantom Hoofs' — criminal and fugitive from the law.

4

Fenella shrank back on her pillows — white as the sheet which she instinctively drew up close round her neck. She tried to be calm and cool.

'Oh, so you have come back in spite of your word,' she said.

'Don't make a noise — don't call anybody. I want to talk to you,' he said.

The light of the match flickered out. Fenella stared through the darkness.

'You had better go away — get out of this room,' she said.

'No. I am going to talk to you . . . ' the voice was decisive. 'Where is your lamp? let me light it.'

'No — go away — at once . . . '

Fenella broke off. The man had lit another match. Once again she saw, by the feeble flare of the little flame, that curiously haunting face of the man called 'Phantom Hoofs.' She saw, too, that he was smiling derisively. He looked quickly about him, found the little parchment-shaded lamp by her bedside, and moved to it. He struck yet another match and lit the lamp. The bedroom was flooded with the soft light. Fenella sat up in her bed, her heart beating frantically fast. She stared at him, wondering what he meant to do.

The man's gaze roved round the room. He seemed to regard it half curiously, half scornfully. It was a luxurious nest which Dick Shaw had prepared for his daughter. A modern room full of lovely things brought out here to the wilds at considerable expense and trouble, with its thick, soft rugs, painted walls, old oak furniture. A delicious disorder of feminine lingerie, and in the air that faint, elusive scent of sweet lilies. The pale blue eyes of the man turned to the shrinking figure of the girl in the bed.

How lovely she was, he thought, her fair curls ruffled over her small head. One bare white shoulder showed over the rim of the sheet which two trembling little hands clutched up to her chin.

'So you are my wife,' said the man whom she knew to be a desperate outlaw. He approached her bed slowly. 'Well, you're much more beautiful than anything I have ever imagined. Can it be true that you *are* my wife? If so — then what they say of me is true. I bear a charmed life and my luck is stupendous!'

He laughed softly and seated himself on the edge of the bed. Fenella, half fainting with terror — edged away from him — then leaned forward to seize her velvet wrapper. But at once he put out a hand and caught her groping fingers. She shivered as she felt the iron grip of them. Looking down, she saw that his hand was like dark mahogany against the lily whiteness of her skin.

'Let me go!' she whispered.

'Ssh — don't raise your voice — don't let anybody hear. Not a soul on earth must know that I am here, tonight.'

She tried to wrench her fingers loose.

'Let me go — or I swear I'll scream — call my servants and give you up.'

'Give me up? Gail O'Shean — your husband? Why give *me* up?' His voice was low, but a look of alarm had entered the blue eyes, which she was quick to see.

'Because I know who and what you are,' she panted. 'You may be Gail O'Shean. But you are also '*Phantom Hoofs*'!'

The man released her instantly. Fenella made a dive for her wrapper and slid her bare arms into it. Her cheeks, her very throat was hot. She was no coward, but it was more than even her strong nerves could stand, that this man should be seated on her bed at dead of night, claiming to be her *husband*.

'So you know — that!' he said.

'Yes, I do. Why didn't you tell me that before you married me?'

'My dear!' he protested, shrugging his shoulders. 'We asked no questions of each other. I married you at your own request.'

'But if I had known . . . '

76

'If you'd known I was 'Phantom Hoofs' — you'd never have done it — eh?' He gave a low, amused laugh, keeping his keen gaze upon her.

'No — I'd never have done it,' said Fenella. 'And in any case, we agreed that we'd never meet again.'

'Ah — you must forgive me — but the memory of you was one a man could not blot out.'

The flattery left her unmoved. Coldly and curiously now she stared at him, this man for whom all Alberta was searching. In the lamplight he seemed changed. He was not the tired, dishevelled rider who had gone through the ceremony of marriage with her, twenty-four hours ago. Not the charming Irishman who had smiled and waved goodbye to her from the saddle. He seemed harder, less human, a ruthless man accustomed to taking desperate measures, without fear of the law. He was a much more *physical* person, this man who sat on the edge of the bed and devoured her with his eyes, and she felt unutterably afraid of him. Yet the fascination of his handsome, light-coloured eyes, set so deeply in his thin face, held her as it had held her in the first hour of their meeting. She was bewildered and dominated by his personality. She managed to say:

'You promised to leave me alone, and you must keep your word. But first you have got to agree to set me free.'

'Set you free! But why? Didn't you marry me to suit your own convenience? Why do you want freedom so quickly?'

'That can't concern you. All I can say is that I made a dreadful mistake, and I want you to sign an agreement to annul our marriage.'

'I'm not sure that I wish to,' he said in a low voice.

Fenella caught her breath.

'But you're mad — you must — you can't do anything else, under the circumstances.'

'Listen,' he said, bending towards her, 'you married me according to the law, and you can't undo it in a second.

You may have discovered that I'm an outlaw, but sure as you sit there, little lady of Bar-None Ranch — you're *my wife*.'

Terror seized her.

'That may be, but you've got to set me free.'

He laughed softly.

'Sorry, darling, but I don't want to. You're much too lovely and desirable.'

His arms suddenly caught her and held her. His hand slipped over the golden head, over the cool white shoulders. His lips crushed hers in a kiss that robbed her of all power to think or move. Half fainting, she heard his voice:

'You belong to me. You can't deny that. *You belong to me!*'

Then Fenella recovered herself. She could not release herself from those steel-like arms, but she knew that she had one sure weapon. Her hand shot out and closed over the bell which hung behind her bed.

'If you don't let me go — immediately — I'll ring this bell,' she said. 'I'll ring it, and have you arrested by the Sheriff — now — this moment.'

He let her go instantly. He seemed to battle for an instant with his passions; then managed to control himself. He stood up.

'As you wish,' he said. 'I'll go at once.'

'I think you had better, Gail O'Shean,' she said, her eyes blazing at him. And she felt suddenly that she loathed him. She had been attracted by him during their strange wedding, but this man whose lips had bruised hers in that brutal kiss was different, and she loathed him.

She sprang out of bed, wrapping her velvet gown about her, and slipped her bare feet into fur moccasins.

'Now,' she said, facing him, 'get out or I'll call my servants and have you arrested.'

'So you'd arrest your own husband?'

Her face whitened.

'I don't want this thing to become public news — otherwise I wouldn't hesitate to put you in gaol. I was out of my mind when I married you, but now my only wish is to annul that marriage as quickly and quietly as possible.'

'And if I refuse?'

'You have no right to refuse,' she said.

'I don't acknowledge 'rights' or 'wrongs'.'

'Then I'll pay you.'

His eyes wavered, then he laughed and shrugged his shoulders.

'Damn it, I'm not sure I don't prefer you to money. You're so beautiful — a fellow can't be blamed for wanting to keep you. I'm half in love with you now, Fenella O'Shean.'

'You don't know what love is. You're an outlaw and a criminal — the sort of swine who doesn't hesitate to rob farmers and terrorise defenceless travellers,' said Fenella. 'It's money you want. Come now — I offer you enough.'

'Oh, very well,' he said softly. '*How* much?'

It was queer how her heart sank like a stone when she heard him say that. She was a woman, and like all women

81

— romantic at heart. She would have preferred 'Phantom Hoofs' to keep to his first statement, that it was she, herself, he wanted rather than money. But no — he was just an avaricious scoundrel. It was money that tempted him. With money she could buy her freedom.

'How much will you take to set me free at once?' she asked.

He reflected a moment.

'I can't decide tonight,' at length he said.

'Why not?' She was in an agony of impatience now to have him gone, and end this impossible situation.

'No,' he said, 'I can't decide it just now. But I'll think things over and — let you know.'

'You'll give me my freedom for a sum to be agreed upon between us?'

'Maybe,' he said, smiling in a queer way.

'But when shall I see you — when will you let me know?'

'I'll come back tomorrow night

— that is, if I can trust you.'

'If you'll keep your hands off me and talk business, I won't give you away.'

He gave a mocking bow.

'I shall find it hard to keep my hands off such a fascinating wife — but since you object . . . '

'I do!' cut in Fenella indignantly.

'Then we'll talk business — tomorrow night.'

'At what time?'

'This time. Midnight. I'll tap on this window.'

Fenella shook her head.

'You can come to my front door.'

'No, thanks. I'll come to this window.

'I have a good mind to let the Sheriff know where to find you,' she said.

He laughed.

'Do that, fair lady, and you will never be free. I shall claim you for my wife when I come out of gaol.'

She shivered and moved back from him.

'Blackmail — worthy of 'Phantom Hoofs',' she said.

He kissed the tips of his fingers to her.

'And a wife worthy of him, too. *Au revoir*, Beautiful. Till this time tomorrow night, and then we shall see what price you are prepared to pay for your freedom.'

She stood speechless, watching him. He climbed over the sill, put the window down softly and was gone. She heard the faint clop-clop of a horse's hoof-beats. He was riding away, clip-clop-clop. *'Phantom Hoofs'?* Gail O'Shean.

Fenella O'Shean sank on the edge of the bed and covered her face with her hands. Why in God's name had she tied herself up to that man just because she had suspected Max of infidelity? Oh, why had she done it? It was Max she loved and wanted — Max loved her, too.

And what possessed her to feel disappointed in that outlaw whose wife she had become? Yet she was. She had rather liked him last night. She had had an almost thrilling remembrance of the way

84

those light Irish eyes had smiled at her from the thin, tired face, and the charm of that wide, sweet smile of his when he had said farewell. But this man who had held her, kissed her so recklessly tonight, she hated and feared.

She dared not tell Max that the outlaw had come back, nor that he was returning tomorrow. But she would pay the price of her freedom and have a document ready for him to sign . . . a paper agreeing to the annulment.

She got back into bed and blew out the lamp. But she was not able to close her eyes in sleep again that night.

In the early hours of the morning, she lay brooding over the affair, and she half made up her mind to tell Max and have him with her when Gail O'Shean came again. She would let Max deal with Gail as he deserved. But she was frustrated in that plan. She received a note that morning, at breakfast time, just a few scribbled lines, brought by a half-breed Indian runner.

'*I will do as you ask, but understand we must be absolutely alone. If you have a third person present, it will mean a bullet through his or her head. I mean this.*

'*Phantom Hoofs.*'

She shivered, and burned this letter.

'Brute,' she thought. 'He would even do murder . . . '

And he was her husband. Had ever a jealous woman made a crazier mistake? She knew she dared not tell Max about her mysterious visit from 'Phantom Hoofs,' It might mean Max's death. No! Alone she had got herself into this tangle, and alone and single-handed she must get herself out of it again.

5

About ten miles away from Bar-None Ranch, hidden under a frowning gorge in the mountains, near the Troit Pass, there was a certain rocky cave which had in earlier days been used by gipsy smugglers. That cave, which had two secret entrances, was still used by desperate fugitives from the law. At this very moment it was the hiding-place of an Irishman named Mike O'Shean — known in Alberta as 'Phantom Hoofs.'

Michael O'Shean, and possibly nobody else in Canada, knew the secret of these entrances to the cave. One was a long, tortuous pathway, tunnelled under the gorge, and coming out the other side upon a swift-flowing river. On more than one occasion when the Sheriff and his men searched the cave, they found no trace of the outlaw, because the secret entrance was blocked up. Fugitives at the other end of the tunnel could swim across the river, and there be supplied by their accomplices with a horse on the other side of the bank.

At the moment, Mike was not occupying his cave alone. When he returned from a certain nocturnal visit to Fenella Shaw, the lady of Bar-None Ranch — he found a light burning in the cave and a man, smoking a pipe, keeping vigil for him. It was his brother Gail. The resemblance between them was so marked that none could tell the difference. They were not twins, but there was only a year between them, and they were both of slim, agile build. Both had thick black hair and a white lock, and those striking blue eyes. Only a mother or woman in love could have detected the differences in the two faces. Gail had more sensitive nostrils, a more tender curve of lip. Mike's face was brutalised. He had been hardened, coarsened by the life he had led in Canada, where he had been evading the law for five years.

When Mike returned to the cave that dark March dawn, he was cold from his ride. But his face wore an almost malicious smile, as though some secret, spiteful thought amused him.

'Where've you been, Mike?' asked Gail. 'I got anxious about you. I'm fagged out. I want to sleep. But while you were out . . . '

'Oh, I'm not dead yet,' broke in the other man. 'I've been a-wooing, that's all.'

'Wooing,' repeated Gail, then laughed curtly. 'I didn't know you had much use for women in your life, Mike, at least not serious use.'

'For women — no. For one woman — yes.'

Gail smoked his pipe in silence. He frowned a little. So Mike was interested in a woman! One woman! Yes, in the life of a man there was always one . . . out-standing one. Gail felt a queer, fierce thrill of his pulses when he remembered the woman whom he had married, secretly, at Bar-None Ranch, the night before last.

He had been quite unable to erase Fenella Shaw from his mind, unable to stamp out the memory of beautiful grey eyes, of a silky fair head and delicate features, and the slim finger on which he had slid a wedding-ring. Fenella O'Shean. His wife! And he had married her . . . in return for a horse and a hundred dollars!

Mike O'Shean looked at his brother slyly.

'Better not tell Gail I've seen his wife tonight,' he thought, 'I think I see a way of making a little money out of this, if I play my cards cunningly. She didn't know the difference between us. Nobody ever did in the old days at home. It's a stroke of luck for me, Gail coming out to Edmonton.'

But Gail O'Shean, brooding over his pipe, was at this very moment asking himself why had he been fool enough to leave England and come to Canada. He had started out with the best of intentions, and had been floundering in a sea of trouble ever since — trouble which he must frankly lay at his brother's door, for it was none of his own.

Mike had always been a trouble-maker, even when they were boys in the old days in Ireland. No school would keep him. Their parents had died when they were of young age, and left them in the hands of an uncle who drank and had little control over either of them. They had had to fend for themselves.

Gail, always with something of the poet and the dreamer in him, wanted education. Utterly different in temperament from Mike, he had settled down to work hard, got a scholarship and entered the University at Dublin.

At twenty-two, he was in a job, managing a big estate for some wealthy landowners in Donegal. But Mike, a year older, was already on the downward grade, got himself mixed up in a political fracas, joined the rebels, was flung in and out of gaol twice and finally vanished from the country.

Then when Ireland was in the teeth

of upheavals, Gail's employers lost their money and had to abandon their estates. Gail forfeited his job. With what little money he had saved he bought himself a farm, but that hadn't brought him any luck. For five years he laboured, and although he loved the soil, he had turned, as was his nature, more to books and dreaming. So that venture failed, and the farm passed into the hands of mortgagees. Gail found himself in London, wondering where his next penny was coming from.

At that psychological moment he had heard from his brother Michael. Mike wrote from Alberta, told Gail that he was working a good ranch and wanted him to go out there and join him.

Glad of this chance, and with the hope that Mike had proved himself some good after all, Gail sailed for Canada. No sooner had he set foot on shore than he had been arrested and flung into gaol. His striking resemblance to his brother had not diminished with the years, and at twenty-eight they were both as alike as two peas in a pod. Gail held his tongue about his identity in order to see how the land lay. It was soon plain to him, much to his bitter disappointment, that Mike was a crook. Mike owned no ranch, neither had he made his money honestly. He was the terror of the lonely ranchers outside Edmonton. He was '*Phantom Hoofs*' . . . a name which struck fear at the heart of women, and which was used as a threat for naughty children.

Gail had always been loyal. There is no more loyal blood in the world than the Irish. He thought if he stuck by Mike now he could make him give up his career of crime. Mike got in touch with Gail and effected his escape from the tiny country lock-up where they had put him, pending an inquiry. And it had been on the night of that escape that Gail had arrived, weary and hounded, at the Bar-None Ranch. And there, for the sake of a horse and money, that he had gone through that amazing marriage with Fenella Shaw.

He had then ridden to the house in Edmonton where Mike lived in disguise, and together the brothers escaped to the cave on the Troit Pass, where Mike said they must remain until the first hue and cry for the escaped prisoner had died down. Then they could slip over the border to another part of Canada. Mike had given Gail his word that he would run straight in future. They would buy a ranch and settle down to work together, he said. And Gail believed him. But Mike had no intention of running straight. He merely hoped to use Gail and their amazing resemblance to each other to further his criminal exploits.

Gail in his frank fashion had told Mike about his marriage to Fenella Shaw. Immediately Mike had thought:

'Gee — the richest dame in Alberta! There ought to be money in this . . . '

Unknown to Gail, he had slipped down to Bar-None Ranch this night, and found out what he wanted to know. That Fenella Shaw regretted her marriage and wanted it annulled. Mike saw money in it, all right.

Unfortunately for Mike and his plans, however, Gail O'Shean was making plans of his own concerning Fenella.

That next day — a cold, brisk day when the sunlight flashed over the glittering, snow-peaked mountains and rapidly thawed the snow that lay over the rough roads twisting round the gorge — Gail spoke of Fenella, while he sat over a rough-and-ready breakfast with his brother.

'Mike,' he said, 'how much longer'll we be in this wretched hole? I've never had to hide my face from any man before, and I don't much like it.'

'All right — don't fuss,' said Mike soothingly. 'We'll get away at dawn tomorrow and ride for the border.'

'At dawn,' said Gail, reflectively.

'Yep. That suit you?'

'Fine — if you swear to keep within the law when we get away, Mike.'

' 'Course I will,' said Mike, his blue eyes full of an honesty which did not exist in him.

'Well, look here,' said Gail, 'you may think me crazy — but I've got to see that girl, Fenella O'Shean as she is now — once more before I quit Alberta.'

Mike's eyes narrowed.

'Oh, I shouldn't if I were you. It isn't safe,' he said.

'But I've got to,' said Gail stubbornly. 'Why?'

Gail's brown face flushed slightly. He stood up and stared down the mountain side in the direction of the pastures where Fenella's herds would be grazing as soon as the thaw set in and the snows melted.

'I can't tell you, Mike, unless it is that I've fallen in love . . . ' He laughed a trifle self-consciously. 'I'm like you, Mike. It isn't *women* with me, collectively . . . it's one individual woman. I can't forget that girl I married down there at Bar-None Ranch, and I've got to see her face once more — if I never see it again on this earth.'

Mike bit his lip. He hadn't bargained for this. Gail had told him he had agreed never to see Fenella again. He didn't want Gail going down there — upsetting his apple-cart. Besides, he had planned to visit the little lady tonight and extract a handsome sum of money from her. He tried to dissuade his brother. He said it was madness, much too dangerous. He might be trapped, captured. It would endanger him, Mike. He argued every way — tried everything. But Gail O'Shean was pig-headed. He had made up his mind to see the girl who was his wife once again . . . and nothing would make him alter it.

'I'll do anything for you — see you through anything, Mike, but I must see — *her* — once more,' he said quietly. 'She's in my blood. That's all. I can't forget her. I've never even touched her lips with mine; perhaps never will. But I want to hear her voice and feel her little hand in mine tonight . . . and I shall do it!'

Mike gnawed at his lip. Here was a pretty kettle of fish and he could say nothing. He dared not tell Gail what a mean, low thing he had done last night, dared not laugh and tell him that *he* had touched Fenella's lips, and felt her slim body shivering with terror in his arms. Gail would be mad if he knew that he had blackmailed her that way, and was after her money now.

He dared not quarrel with Gail, either. He was too useful to him just now, when his position with the police was desperate. So he had to hold his tongue.

So that night soon after midnight — it was not Mike, the ruthless, the brutal, the true 'Phantom Hoofs,' who tapped on Fenella's window-pane. It was Gail O'Shean — who had never done a crooked thing in his life and never wanted to do one.

He was Fenella's husband . . . and he was a man in love . . . in love with a dream . . . the dream of the marriage he had contracted with her . . . the memory of her haunting face and soft hands and Celtic charm.

He was surprised to find that this signal on her window was answered at once. Fenella drew the curtains and admitted him without argument. Almost as though she expected him, he thought, because she was fully dressed and had a fur coat about her shoulders. His heart seemed to turn over at the sight of her. The most intense and passionate desire to touch her shot through him. He reached out a hand and said:

'Fenella . . . '

But no other words came. They froze on his lips. Gail found himself staring into the shining barrel of an automatic which Fenella was levelling at him. Her voice, cold and stern, said:

'If you lay a finger on me, tonight, I shall shoot. I know now what you are, and I've got to protect myself. This is a business discussion, and that is what it'll remain. Now — come in!'

6

Gail stared at Fenella, dumbfounded. Why should she be threatening him with a revolver, and why did she say that she *knew who he was?* She had known nothing about him on the night that he had married her.

'Come in, if you are coming,' repeated Fenella in her curt, cold young voice.

Slowly, Gail climbed over the sill. He stared round him, strangely embarrassed by the sight of this pretty, feminine bedroom. Yet his heart thrilled at the faint, intriguing perfume of lilies in the air. Her perfume. So well he remembered it. It had clung about her on that night of their marriage. Was it possible, he asked himself, with pulses that suddenly raced, that she was really, legally, his wife? She was so lovely and lissom and worth a man's loving. There was all the beauty and sorrow of Ireland in her eyes. The Ireland for which he was strangely homesick, out here in Canada. His wife! It must be a dream, and such dreams never came true.

He had expected to find her in bed . . . perhaps scared a little . . . resentful a little, because he had come. He had meant to reassure her, touch her slender fingers, perhaps kiss her once . . . leave her, never to see her again.

But nothing like that materialised.

Fenella was fully dressed in a woollen jersey and thick suède skirt. Her furs were keeping out the cold of the frosty night. She bade him to follow her into the next room. She had no intention of another awkward, terrifying scene such as she had had last night.

In the sitting-room there was a log-fire, and it was warm and homely and very desirable to Gail, who was tired and chilled from his long ride. A shaded lamp burned on the desk. Fenella went straight to this desk and picked up a sheet of foolscap. Then she turned to Gail, the revolver still pointing at him.

'I have the papers here, all ready,' she said.

'What papers?' he asked, astonished.

Fenella flushed.

'Don't try and pretend you know nothing about it. I told you clearly last night — you must agree to annul our marriage.'

'You — told me — *last night?*' he echoed.

She made an impatient gesture with one slim hand.

'Don't waste time. Let's get this business fixed. How much money do you want in return for my freedom?'

He came a step nearer her. She immediately backed away.

'I swear I'll put a bullet through you if you touch me . . . ' she said.

He could only stand still and stare. He was astounded by her manner and her words. Why was she so terrified of him? What did she mean by all this talk of last night?

'Listen,' he said. 'This wants a bit of explanation, as far as I am concerned. What are you so scared of? What do you think I'm going to do?'

Her lips quivered slightly. Her lashes fluttered.

'You — you behaved like a beast — last night. I'm not going to risk it happening again,' she said.

'*I — behaved like a beast — last night?*'

'Yes.'

'But, my dear,' he said quietly, 'you are either dreaming, or a little crazy, because I was not here last night.'

It was her turn to stare. Then she gave a quick, nervous laugh.

'That's a lie, Gail O'Shean.'

'No, I am not lying to you — Mrs. Gail O'Shean!'

He smiled and uttered the last words tenderly.

Fenella was as astounded now as the man. She drew closer to him and stared into his face. This was Gail O'Shean all right, the man she had married, the man who had terrorised her last night. Unmistakable, with his thin face redeemed from insignificance by the strikingly handsome eyes which were as blue as pale forget-me-nots under the strongly-marked brows. Yet . . . he was different tonight. Subtly, strangely different. He was more like the man she remembered on that crazy night of her wedding. Attractive, curiously disarming. His voice was different from the rougher voice of last night. That smile, a tender and charming one — that was the smile of the Irishman she had married and remembered without rancour.

Yet last night she had loathed and feared him, and he had insulted her.

'Who came here last night?' he asked her. 'Because I assure you, I did not.'

Very slowly Fenella let fall the hand that levelled the revolver at him.

'I don't understand you,' she said. 'Do you mean to tell me you didn't come here and bully me . . . that you didn't arrange to come back tonight and sign this paper of annulment in return for money?'

'I did not,' he said.

'But you did — *you did*!' she panted. 'I know that you did. Unless . . . ' she added with an hysterical laugh, ' . . . you have a double!'

Then — like a lightning flash — the truth struck Gail. The blood stung his brown weary face. His lips tightened.

'Mike,' he said to himself. 'Of all the damnable tricks . . . *it was Mike*!'

He knew then that his brother had come here and done these things, said these things to Fenella last night. He put two and two together. Mike had returned to the Pass in a peculiar mood. He had said something about 'wooing a woman.' God, but how dared he? Bitterly, now, did Gail regret having told Mike about Fenella. He might have realised that Mike wasn't straight — couldn't run straight. Mike had taken advantage of that knowledge to try to blackmail Fenella, and he had insulted her, into the bargain.

Any affection Gail had ever had for

his brother died in that hour. Any hope he had entertained of making him give up his life of crime. Gail looked down into the beautiful face of the girl he had married and who had haunted his thoughts ever since.

'You ask me,' he said, 'if I have a double. You are right, I have. And it was he, and not I, who came here last night.'

For an instant Fenella did not believe him.

'You're lying to me.'

'No. I am speaking the truth.'

'You are 'Phantom Hoofs' — the outlaw.'

'No. I am Gail O'Shean. 'Phantom Hoofs', the outlaw, is my brother, Michael, though nobody knows his name. He has no name, to the police, except 'Phantom Hoofs'.'

Fenella put a hand to her head. It was hot and the blood beat in her temples. Could this be true? Was it possible that two men could be so alike? Yet now she was noticing another thing.

The man who had come last night had worn the rough clothes of a rancher. This man was attired in the well-cut English riding breeches and coat which he had worn when she had first seen him. His face was amazingly alike to that of the man who had tried to blackmail her. Yet she could see now that it was different. More refined of feature, more tender in expression. These lips looked as though they could be kind and sensitive as well as passionate.

'Can it be possible?' she whispered. 'Two men — so alike?'

'We are brothers,' said Gail. 'I didn't mean anybody in Canada to know. I wanted to help Mike . . . I meant to be loyal to him. But since you have been so rottenly treated — I don't see why I should let you think *I'm* the swine. You must believe me, Fenella — I'm Gail O'Shean, and the fellow who came last night — is my brother, Mike.'

Fenella's beautiful eyes searched his. Some instinct told her that he spoke the truth. She laid the revolver down on the table. A curious feeling of relief, of warmth, stole over her. She was glad . . . yes, glad . . . that she was not the wife of that other man, that brute, that criminal. She knew definitely that she was not afraid of *this* man. She would have no need to use her revolver tonight.

She moved to the fireplace and sat down in a chair. She was trembling.

'Will you tell me — everything?' she said.

Gail told her all that had happened since he had left England and been arrested on his arrival in Alberta, in mistake for his brother.

When he had finished, Fenella nodded her head.

'I understand now,' she said.

'You believe me?'

'Absolutely. I *feel* — in spite of the amazing resemblance, physically, between you, that you and Mike O'Shean are not the same.'

His light blue eyes suddenly sparkled.

'Be careful, mavourneen . . . I may be lying . . . I may be a cunning rogue.'

She looked straight into his eyes and shook her head.

'No. You are — not 'Phantom Hoofs'.'

'You are right. I am just — Gail O'Shean.'

'You told your brother you were coming here tonight?'

'Yes. He tried to talk me out of it.'

'I see. He was baffled. He meant to come and get the money himself.'

'He'll get no mercy or forgiveness from me for this.'

'What I don't understand is why you came tonight? You promised never to see me again.'

Gail did not answer for a moment. He let his gaze rest on her and felt every nerve tingling with a strange mixture of joy and pain. Such a brief while ago he had not cared whether a girl named Fenella lived or died. She had been outside his scheme of things. But he had found her memory haunting him . . . stirring him to remembrance of her beauty, her charm; and the tragedy that had lain in her eyes when she had asked him to marry her. He had known that, despite himself, he had fallen in love with her in that hour. He knew, looking at her tonight, that he loved her to madness, that he would give anything on earth to make their marriage a real one.

'What made you come back?' she asked again.

He moved slowly toward her.

'I wanted to see you again,' he said.

'Why?'

'Because at dawn tomorrow, I was supposed to ride over the border into safety with my brother. I knew I'd probably never set eyes on you again. I felt that I *must* see you once more. That's all.'

Her heart gave a queer throb. She stood up and found herself looking up into his eyes. Irish eyes that were full of passionate hunger. Yet she was not afraid as she had been last night . . . only unaccountably stirred.

'Surely it wasn't to see me,' at length she said, 'it was for money — you wanted money . . . '

'Be quiet, Fenella O'Shean,' he cut in. 'I don't want your money and you know it. You lent me a hundred dollars last time we met. I've brought it back.'

He put his hand in his pocket, drew out a roll of bills and tossed them on to the desk beside her. She looked at them, then back at him. Her own face flamed with colour.

'Then *why* — did you want to — to see me?'

'Because I've fallen in love with my wife.'

Fenella put a hand to her lips.

'You're quite crazy.'

'Crazy — because I've fallen in love?'

'You don't know me. We're strangers.'

'I've seen you — the beauty of you — the wonder of you. I've touched your hand. I've put a ring on your finger. You've taken it off. But that can't annul our marriage. Fenella, the law made us man and wife. That was enough. Now I know I adore you — every hair of your head — that I'd give my life to serve you — stay with you — for ever!'

She stood dumbfounded. His low, intense voice had strange witchery in it, stirred her to the depths of her being. Here was no brutal outlaw, gloating over her . . . here was a real lover, declaring his love, a man whose gaze could rest on her lips and make her feel he had touched them in a kiss.

She was curiously unafraid of him. But her face and throat were rosy red. She tried to be angry — to think of Max.

'You don't know what you're saying,' she stammered. 'It's impossible. You — you must go away as you meant to, and never see me again.'

'You don't care whether I live or die?'

'Why should I?'

'No — you only used me to your own ends on the night you married me.'

'I served a purpose for you, too,' she reminded him.

112

'Yes. You gave me a horse and possibly saved me from imprisonment in the place of my brother. But you did me a wrong, Fenella — you did not know it, but, my dear, you've filled me with torment . . . a torment of longing for you, mavourneen, which will never leave me till I die.'

She clasped both hands over her pounding heart. She tried to remember Max . . . her lover, whom she loved. Was she crazy that she should allow herself to be thrilled and moved by this man? Yet somehow, the things he said in that Irish voice of his, the way he looked at her lips, penetrated all her reticence, and found the warm, responsive woman in her. She was afraid now, not of him, *but of herself.*

'Gail O'Shean, this is crazy talk,' she said. 'You must go away and forget our marriage. I have papers here for you to sign. Our marriage must be annulled.'

'Why? What's made you change your mind so rapidly?'

'I made a mistake,' she said. 'I thought

Max Geering — my fiancé — had played the fool with my Indian maid. I know now that he had not. I want my freedom — so that I can marry him.'

Silence for a moment. The spruce logs leaped and crackled in the open fireplace. Gail O'Shean looked down at the beautiful face of the girl and his heart seemed to turn to stone within him. So she loved this Max Geering, whoever he was. She no longer wanted to get away from him. She believed in him again.

'I see,' he said. 'You want your freedom so that you can marry — this other chap.'

'Yes, yes, and you must give it to me. I . . . told your brother . . . I'd pay anything . . . within reason.'

Gail's eyes narrowed.

'I don't want money. Get that into your head.'

'But you will sign the papers . . . agree to the annulment, won't you?' she asked feverishly.

The loveliness, the grace of her, and

the knowledge that she was, legally, his wife, mounted suddenly to his head. Before she could speak again he reached her side and drew her into his arms. He held her as though he could never let her go again. His eyes burned down into hers.

'You don't know what you ask me,' he said. 'There's something in you that draws me like a magnet . . . some fire that burns me. I'm burnt up with longing for you. Fenella, Fenella, you are my wife . . . and I don't want to let you go!'

She lay silent in his impassioned embrace. The room seemed to spin round her. What was it about this man that moved her and excited her so? Last night, when Mike O'Shean, pretending to be her husband, had told her he wanted her, she had been furious — she had loathed him. But she was not furious with Gail . . . neither did she loathe him. There was a strange sincerity, a beauty, a truth behind his passion which stirred her to the depths of her being.

Then she thought of Max and was ashamed.

'Let me go,' she whispered. 'Let me go — please.'

Just for an instant Gail O'Shean's lips touched the fairness of her hair. She felt his strong body shaking. Then he released her.

'I am sorry,' he said. 'You're my wife . . . and yet I have no right . . . '

'I am sorry, too,' she said, 'but you must see — it's impossible. I . . . I'm in love with this other man.'

'Are you sure of that, Fenella — and of him?'

'Yes.'

'I see . . . ' Gail gave a short, tired laugh. He looked down at her with hopeless longing. Taking one of her hands, he kissed it — kissed every finger, slowly, one by one.

'I wish to God I'd never known you and never been led into marriage with you,' he said. 'Because you are in my blood like a fever, and I shall never cure myself of you, now.'

She drew her fingers away, baffled and perplexed by the emotion he roused in her. He added slowly:

'Fenella O'Shean — I shall not ride at dawn with Mike. Neither shall I sign those papers tonight and give you your freedom.'

'Why?'

'Because I'm going to ask you for something . . . set my *own* price on your freedom.'

'What is it?' she asked breathlessly.

'Not money,' said Gail O'Shean with a slow, strange smile. 'But I would like a memory of you to take with me through my lifetime — and beyond into the grave. I want one hour with you, my wife. After that we need never meet again.'

Scarlet and confused, she looked back at him.

'One hour — with you. You mean . . . '

'I mean I shall not harm you, acushla,' he said gently. 'You need not be afraid. But let me come back here, at this hour tomorrow. Just for an hour — let me hold you once in my arms.

Let me know, once, the sweetness of your lips. Then — you can be rid of me for ever.'

Oh, crazy! One madness after another, she thought. Impossible! And yet . . . how could she refuse? She wanted Max and her freedom. She must pay whatever price, within reason, that Gail O'Shean asked — she knew that he would not annul their marriage unless she consented.

'You won't sign now — go away now?' she began.

'No,' he said, 'I ask for one hour — with you, my wife.'

His wife! She felt herself shivering nervously, and her gaze faltered before the hunger and fire in his eyes.

'Very well,' she whispered. 'Come back — tomorrow . . . and I'll keep my word — if you will be reasonable.'

'I promise that, and I'll keep mine. And can I rely on you not to betray me to my brother?'

'Yes.'

'Then — till tomorrow — good

night. Tomorrow you will be rid of me. For tonight — you are still — *my wife*!'

His rich Irish voice lingered on those words, held her in a strange thrall. But he did not touch her hand again. Before she realised it — he was gone.

She stared at the doorway and into the shadows beyond.

'Max!' she whispered. 'Oh, Max!'

She called on that name, almost as though it were a mascot . . . a charm against evil. She felt evil. She must be wanton, she thought, to allow Gail O'Shean's voice and eyes to intoxicate her in this fashion. She began to wish she had not promised to give him that hour tomorrow. It made her unhappy and afraid. Yet despite her love for Max Geering, she could not help the sensation that she *wanted to see* Gail O'Shean once again before he went out of her life for ever.

'Of course, I *am* mad!' she thought.

Yet, it was a madness which did not pass.

Outside the sitting-room door, Talooka,

the Indian maid, had been crouching with an eye to the keyhole, and ears strained. She had seen and understood only enough to convince her that this man, who visited her mistress at dead of night, was 'Phantom Hoofs' — the outlaw. She had not heard Gail's story of his brother. The big black eyes of Talooka sparkled with malice when she saw him take Fenella in his arms.

This would interest the Master . . . and he would no doubt reward her for carrying the news to him.

At dawn, whilst Fenella lay sleeping — exhausted by the emotional scene through which she had passed — Talooka visited Max Geering, manager of Bar-None Ranch, and told him all that she had seen and heard.

7

Another midnight came.

Fenella — believing herself to be the only one awake in a quiet, sleeping household — waited for Gail O'Shean, in the strangest condition of mind. At one moment she dreaded his coming, was terrified of what he might ask of her during the one hour which she had promised him. In another she wanted nothing but to see him again. And, of course, she told herself, she was most anxious for him to sign that paper of annulment and be gone.

She had spent a boring day. Max had visited her. He had been his most charming. He had spoken with sadness and longing of their delayed wedding. And she had stroked that big blond head of his and told herself that she adored him ... that she wanted nothing, nobody but him on earth.

But was that strictly true? If so, why wasn't it Max who occupied her mind all day? Instead she had found herself thinking of Gail O'Shean . . . remembering the blueness of his eyes, the tender, yet passionate curve of his lip. He had never kissed her. Tonight he would kiss her, and she was not afraid. All day she had worried about him, and then been aghast with herself for the treachery of her own emotions. She was mad and bad and disloyal to her poor Max.

'It will be a good thing when Gail O'Shean is gone out of my life for ever,' she told herself feverishly while she awaited him. For Gail O'Shean was so much more like the lover of her girlish imagination than Max Geering could ever be.

At length Gail O'Shean came — softly, through her bedroom window and into the sitting-room.

She stood there, by the fireplace . . . and his dream of her came true again.

She was all ivory and rose and golden with her shining curls, her grey, limpid eyes, her white skin. Tonight she wore a velvet dress, black velvet, and her furs, and Gail O'Shean thought he had never seen such loveliness.

He came slowly toward her.

'All day long I've thought of you,' he said simply.

The blood rushed to her face and throat. She stood half-embarrassed, half-ashamed of herself.

'All day — I've tried to resign myself to setting you free,' he added.

'But you must,' said Fenella.

'I shall keep my word, if you keep yours.'

'Does your — your brother know you have come?'

'Yes. My brother and I have fallen out,' said Gail grimly. 'I told him exactly what I thought of him for trying to blackmail you in my name, and I put my fist between his eyes. He won't forget it. We're parting company when we get over the border tomorrow.'

'I'm glad,' said Fenella.

'Do you care — what becomes of me?' asked Gail with sudden passion in his voice.

'I — I don't want you to — be what *he* is,' she said.

He walked up to her, took her hand, and led her to the sofa which was at right-angles to the fire. He pushed her gently on to it, then sat beside her, keeping her cold hand in his warm, strong fingers.

'One hour — one little hour — to remember all my life,' he said in a low voice. 'Fenella, you witch, would to God I'd never seen your face!'

Her heart fluttered in her breast. She tried to keep calm, to remember Max, to resent what this man said to her. But she could do none of these things. What was it about this man that appealed to her so irresistibly?

'Sweetheart,' said Gail O'Shean, 'will you kiss me, just once, of your own free will?'

She tried to draw her hand away.

'This is crazy ... I ... I love Max Geering ... '

'Are you sure?'

'Yes, sure.'

'You could not love me?'

'How could I?'

'If there had been no Max — could you have loved me?' persisted the low, beguiling voice.

She scarcely dared look at him. She grew hot and then cold. One of the pearls in her ears came loose and fell on to the floor.

'My ear-ring — let me — pick it — up,' she stammered.

'Answer me first — *could you have loved me?*'

'I — oh — let me go,' she said in a suffocated voice.

But Gail O'Shean was a man, and he could not be blind to what lay in the grey eyes of this girl from his own country. He caught her in his arms, held close to his heart, and hid his face against her soft breast.

'My wife ... just for one hour ... oh

God, Fenella, I love you — I love you. Sure and I've forgotten everything on earth but that I love you. Kiss me of your own free will, won't you, my sweet, my sweet!'

She trembled from head to foot. Scarcely knowing what she did, caught in the meshes of a strange enchantment from which she could not escape, she lay against him, knowing that throughout all her love affair with Max there had never been a moment like this. Max had never, could never make her feel as this man was doing. She caught fire from Gail and instinctively lifted her face. His burning lips covered hers, pressed them in a kiss that seemed, mysteriously, to separate her for ever from Max Geering — to unite her to this man and alter the whole of her destiny.

Then — suddenly — into that lamp-lit room — chaos. The door burst open. Gail O'Shean released Fenella, and they sprang to their feet. Two men came into the room. Gail knew neither.

But Fenella, white-lipped, terrified, recognised one as Max and the other as the Sheriff. Both of them carried revolvers and had Gail covered in an instant.

Max smiled reassuringly at Fenella.

'It's all right, darling — we've got the swine now,' he said.

'What does this mean, Max?' she gasped.

The Sheriff laid a hand on Gail's shoulder.

'I arrest you, in the name of the law,' he said. 'So, 'Phantom Hoofs' — we've got you again. And this time, we won't let you go, my fine fellow, as you'll see!'

Gail O'Shean, grey and drawn, stared into the barrel of that revolver, then turned to Fenella. His eyes were terrible.

He said:

'So you broke your word of honour. This was your way of tricking me — with a kiss — Fenella!'

She understood. He thought that she

had betrayed him, that she was responsible for his arrest. She tried to speak, to explain, but no words came. A mist blotted out his grey, accusing face. Then Max caught her in his arms.

8

Fenella's faint was short-lived. She struggled back to consciousness to find herself lying on the couch in her drawing-room with Max kneeling beside her, chafing her hands.

She started up wildly.

'Gail . . . ' she gasped.

Max Geering's eyes narrowed to slits. So that was how the land lay! Fenella called this 'Phantom Hoofs' by his Christian name, and was inclined to be sentimental about him. He had caught sight of her in the man's arms just as he had led the Sheriff into this room. But he was determined not to let Fenella see that he noticed that. He did not wish to precipitate a row between this girl and himself. He wanted her too badly . . . wanted her, and all that she possessed! He would pretend he had seen and heard nothing. He tried to take her in his arms.

'*Liebling* — hush — don't worry — the swine is in custody — in safe hands. He won't be able to hurt you now. I'm here with you, my beloved — your Max who worships you!'

Fenella put a hand to her forehead. It was wet. The silver fair curls were disordered. Her eyes held a bewildered look. She tried to collect her thoughts; she wished somehow that Max would let her go. His caresses did not comfort her, neither was the touch of his hands agreeable to her. She was in a strange state of body and mind, she thought. She was in a thrall — possessed by the memory of the man she had married — Gail O'Shean — Gail, who was *not* 'Phantom Hoofs', the outlaw — but his brother. She was haunted by the thrilling memory of him and their first long kiss.

'*My wife . . . mine . . . just for an hour . . .*' he had said.

She ought to have hated him. But his words, his embrace, had had an amazing, incredible effect upon her. She was ashamed, but could not tear the memory of him from her mind. And she hated the knowledge that he had been captured by Max and the Sheriff. He had thought *her* guilty of betraying him.

His last look had scared her. And now he was gone. He, Gail O'Shean, was going to prison in place of his brother Mike. But she could not tell them all that he was not 'Phantom Hoofs.' She had given her word never to tell them that.

'Fenella, my darling, tell me he didn't hurt you!' she heard Max's voice in her ear.

She tried to collect her scattered wits. She closed her eyes.

'No — he — didn't hurt me.'

'Did he sign the papers of annulment?'

'No — he — hadn't time.'

'He shall do it,' said Max through his teeth. 'You belong to me. You shall not stay as the wife of that criminal.'

Fenella opened her eyes and looked

at Max. Her face was no longer pale. It was burning.

'Max,' she said, 'how did you — know that — that he was coming here tonight?'

'Never mind. I knew.'

'But *nobody* knew except myself.'

'I found out. *Ach,* my dearest — what does it matter? He is a stranger to you, and you must loathe the thought of him. You will be glad you will soon be rid of him. Then we can marry. Look at me, *liebling* — what is worrying you? You still want to marry me — don't you?'

'Yes — of — course,' she said slowly.

Their eyes met. Max's expression was one of the most passionate sincerity. No woman could have doubted him. He looked youthful and eager and healthily handsome, with his ruddy face, blue, smiling eyes, his blond German head. Fenella was suddenly ashamed for having allowed Gail O'Shean's strange, over-powering personality to come between her and her lover. She felt disloyal and mean. She threw herself into Max's arms in her warm, impulsive way.

'Oh, Max, Max — it's all such a ghastly mistake! If only I had never doubted you. Hold me fast . . . don't let me go . . . darling Max!'

The man's heart leapt with triumph. He felt he had won her back. He covered her face with kisses.

'You'll soon belong to me utterly,' he whispered. 'I've forgiven you for doubting me — don't let it trouble you, *liebling*. Forget it.'

She lay quiet in his arms, but did not respond to his kisses. Somehow she could not. She allowed him to do the love-making. But she knew that although she might marry Max and forget that she had doubted him, she could never forget that she had married Gail O'Shean. She wished to God he did not believe that she had betrayed him. She was essentially honest and honourable and true to her word. She could not bear that Gail O'Shean should think that she had set Max and the Sheriff on his track. Even if she never saw him again in this life, she wanted him to know that she was guiltless of such treachery.

And he would be put into gaol — punished in Mike O'Shean's place. That wasn't fair. It was all wrong. What could she do? Nothing, but hope that he would escape — and ride, as he had intended, over the border, into safety.

She felt, suddenly, terribly tired. She drew away from Max's arms.

'Go now, my dear,' she said. 'It's very late — after midnight — you *must* go.'

He stood up and looked down at her, frowning a little. He wanted to question her, to find out exactly when and how she had arranged tonight's meeting with 'Phantom Hoofs,' and what her real sentiments were toward the man. But he dared not probe too deeply into the thing. Under the circumstances, he reflected, holding his peace would pay in the end. He would pretend that nothing had happened. He would win this girl back . . . completely . . . make her love him as she used to do. He was fairly sure of her now. Whatever he did, he could not afford to lose her — the wealthy young owner of the Bar-None Ranch. All his life, Geering had coveted a ranch like this . . . and, in his physical fashion, he was in love with Fenella.

He stayed, smoking and talking with her for a while. Then he took his departure.

'I'll see you tomorrow, my lovely one.'

Fenella made herself kiss him.

'Yes — good night,' she said wearily.

He strolled out of the bungalow, the habitual cigarette between his lips. On the porch out of the shadows stole the slender figure of Talooka, the Indian girl. Her brown eyes sparkled up at him in the starlight. Away to the east the sky was growing light. Another hour and dawn would be breaking.

'Master pleased with Talooka?' she murmured.

He caught one of her black braids and pulled her carelessly towards him.

'Yes, you did well to come to me . . . a good night's work, my little squaw. What reward would you like?'

The Indian girl sidled up to him and lifted her face.

'Talooka marry Tomasso soon, but Talooka love Max . . . all her life . . . '

The man, inordinately vain, was flattered. He cast a swift, furtive look round. Fenella had retired to her bedroom. The Sheriff and his men had gone, driven 'Phantom Hoofs' to the local cells. Max was alone under the stars with Talooka. He breathed in her ear :

'Walk with me now . . . a little way . . . '

Joyously she assented. They disappeared together into the shadows. And in her bedroom, crouching by her bed, Fenella reproached herself for one single moment of disloyalty to Max.

'He is true to me — I ought to be ashamed of myself for thinking about that other man,' she told herself. 'Max, my dear, I'll make up for it, when I am your wife. I'll forget Gail O'Shean — wipe him utterly from my memory.'

But she could not. All that night, sleeping fitfully, she was haunted by the thought of Gail. She was filled with a strange desire to see him again and make him understand that not she, but somebody else, had betrayed him . . . that whatever she did, she would not break a given word.

The crisp, cold morning broke. Fenella awoke early and rang her bell. She needed her tea. Her head ached and she felt nervy, not in her usual splendid health. As a rule, her little Indian maid answered that bell at once. But this morning, Minna — an older half-breed servant — came in.

'Where is Talooka?' asked Fenella, surprised.

The woman shook her head.

'No one tell, my Lady. Not here.'

Fenella questioned her further and was told that none of the other maids had seen Talooka this morning. They thought maybe she had risen early and gone to meet Tomasso, because tomorrow she was leaving domestic service and going to her own people for her marriage.

Fenella thought no more about it. With Minna's help she dressed quickly in riding-shirt and breeches. She looked rather like a boy with her short, curly hair and her extreme slenderness. She was going to ride over to the Sheriff's office. She wanted to know what they had done with the man they believed to be 'Phantom Hoofs.' She thought that perhaps she might see him for an instant. His unexpected arrest last night had upset her incredibly. She was in a bad state of nerves this morning, half-ashamed of the fact, but unable to conquer it.

She ate a poor breakfast, then put on a short leather coat and walked out on to the porch. Her horse was being saddled and brought round to her. She stood a moment, shading her eyes from the sun and looking towards Max's bungalow. She felt half-tender, half-remorseful about Max. She loved him, and he worshipped her. When they were married, the memory of this other business would be blotted out. They would be ideally happy on this ranch, managing it hand in hand, as they had often planned and dreamed.

Then she saw two figures running towards her from her manager's bungalow. As they drew nearer, she looked at them uneasily. They were ranchers, both in her employ. Something appeared to be wrong.

'What's happened now?' Fenella wondered.

The men reached her and saluted respectfully. Fenella addressed the older of the two ranchers.

'What is it, Bob?'

'Please, miss,' said the man breathlessly, ''tis a terrible bit of news we must give you.'

Her heart seemed to stand still.

'What is it, Bob?' she repeated.

'Mr. Geering, miss.'

'Max? What's happened to him?' Fenella put a hand to her lips.

'He — he's been knifed, miss,' said the cowboy called Bob, scarcely daring to look at her.

'*Knifed!*' repeated Fenella. 'My God, do you mean — he — he's . . .'

'He isn't dead, miss — but he's very bad. We thought we'd best come for you.'

'Oh, yes, yes, of course,' said Fenella. 'But, Bob, how did this happen? Who did it?'

'Tomasso,' was the reply.

'*Tomasso?*' Fenella's lips, pale and dry, echoed the name.

'Yes. He gave himself up after he had done it. He's up there now, in the manager's bungalow, under arrest.'

'But why did Tomasso knife Mr. Geering?'

Fenella had started to run towards Max's home and the cowboys kept pace with her. They exchanged significant glances which she did not see. Bob muttered:

'Dunno, I'm sure, miss.'

Fenella's brain refused to work. She only knew that Max had been knifed by Tomasso, her faithful and most-trusted servant. Max, perhaps, was dying. And he was her future husband. He had meant everything in the world to her.

They reached Max's bungalow. All was chaos there. Men everywhere, horses tethered to the trees by the porch, women and children rushing about. Everybody seemed to have reached here before Fenella. As the slim figure of the young owner of the ranch appeared, the crowd fell back and made way for her. Fenella rushed into the bungalow. In the living-room she paused, her heart pounding. She saw her lover lying on the floor. His head was on a pillow, his face ghastly. An Edmonton doctor knelt beside him. Fenella's horrified gaze took in every-thing — the cotton-wool, rolls of bandages — a bowl of water stained to a red, sinister hue.

Fenella gave a cry.

'Oh, Max — darling . . . '

He did not open his eyes, did not answer. The doctor, who had attended Dick Shaw, and knew his daughter slightly, looked up at her and answered her unspoken question.

'He'll be all right, Miss Fenella. It's a nasty wound — just missed the heart by a few inches — but it isn't fatal.'

'Oh, thank God,' she said. Then she swung round. Her eyes glazed as she saw Tomasso, the Chippewayan, standing between two of the Sheriff's men. She walked up to him.

'So, Tomasso,' she said, 'you did this! You tried to murder Mr. Geering! You knew that I am going to marry him. What have I ever done to deserve this from you? I have always treated you well and fairly since you have worked for me on my ranch, and my father trusted you.'

Tomasso was standing like a bronze statue, his arms folded across his chest. He looked down into her eyes without flinching.

'You have treated me well and fairly, my Lady,' he said. 'But Mr. Geering has not treated you or me well and fairly, so I tried to kill him.'

'Why do you say that, Tomasso?'

'At dawn,' said Tomasso in a cold,

clear voice, 'I find Talooka, who was to marry me — in arms of Mr. Geering. They make love. For a long time they make love. So — I watch. I try to kill him.'

Silence. Fenella stood still, staring at the man. Her face changed from burning scarlet to white. She felt suddenly, physically sick.

'It isn't true,' she said. '*It isn't true.*'

'It is true, my Lady,' said Tomasso.

Fenella swung round. She looked down at Max, who was still unconscious of her presence. She looked, as through a mist, down at his handsome, familiar face. And she recalled that evening when she had surprised him here, when she had found Talooka in his bedroom and he had looked so guilty, so angry. Yet he had denied everything. So had the girl.

She shivered from head to foot. She felt humiliated before all these, her men . . . who knew that her future husband had betrayed her for an Indian servant.

'You are mistaken, Tomasso,' she said.

'Talooka will tell you, it is not true.'

Then a slender figure in a fringed dress crept out of a corner and flung itself down at Fenella's feet. Talooka, trembling, terrified, her face bathed in tears.

'My Lady — forgive Talooka. It *is* true. But she love Max much. He try to force her marry Tomasso ... so my Lady should not know.'

Another horrible silence. Nobody dared look at Fenella. But she knew, now, indubitably, that Max was unfaithful. Her pride and faith crumpled up. She looked blindly at the Indian girl who crouched, sobbing, at her feet. Then, wordlessly, Fenella turned and walked out of the bungalow.

9

At dawn, that same morning, Gail
O'Shean paced the floor of the local
'lock up' in the Sheriff's dwelling, five
miles from the Bar-None Ranch. He
had been conveyed there after his arrest
the previous night. Later, he knew he
would be taken to Edmonton, and once
there, in the hands of the police, he
would be doomed. As 'Phantom Hoofs'
he would be sentenced to a long term
of imprisonment for a variety of crimes.

Gail's thin face was strained and
tired, but his eyes, his lips, were
granite-hard. One thing in this world he
could neither tolerate nor forgive.
Treachery. Fenella's conduct had been
the very epitome of treachery, this
night. He had come to her, asking for
one hour with her, one little hour
before he went on his way, never to see
her again. He had promised to annul

their marriage. And she had given her word that she would meet him alone and that not a soul in Alberta should ever know that he had visited her.

She had been so gentle, so unexpectedly yielding in his arms. He had felt her trembling against him. She had seemed more lovely than a dream, and he had felt a great rush of emotion for her, unlike anything he had ever experienced or expected to feel. But her sweetness had been merely to decoy him. She had arranged for that yellow-haired German fellow, and the Sheriff, to steal in upon them and make the arrest.

Somehow Gail would have staked his life that Fenella was finer than that, a woman whom a man might respect. Well, he had been a fool. He had no respect left for her. He despised her. But at the same time he could not forget the rapture of their embrace, and that feeling that he had gained the whole world. He, Gail O'Shean, had been made a fool of — and nothing would suffice now but that he paid that girl back. Well, *did he not hold her in the hollow of his hand?* She was his wife. She would remain his wife. He would never set her free. That good-looking German fellow, with his swagger and his arrogance, was her lover, was he? She wanted her freedom so that she could marry him? Well, she would never do it now. She was *his* wife. She was Fenella O'Shean, and one day — if he had to wait years — he would claim her. And the next time her slim, beautiful body trembled in his arms, he would not let her go.

Up and down the cell he paced, all through the dark hours until the cold March dawn broke over the country-side. Outside the door there was a man on sentry, and the small barred window was not large enough to allow a man to squeeze through. Gail looked about him grimly and recognised the fact that he could not escape.

He wondered if Fenella would break her other promise, that she would not tell a soul that he was the brother of

'Phantom Hoofs.' That would either complicate matters or not be believed. Gail could not tell what would happen. But he felt suddenly that it was unfair that he should bear Mike's punishment for him. Mike had behaved badly — particularly where Fenella was concerned. Why should Mike get over the border into safety whilst he, who was innocent, served his sentence?'

Swift resentment gripped Gail O'Shean by the throat. He could not forget Fenella. His wife! God, he hated her and desired her — both. He felt in this hour, that he would like to press his fingers on that beautiful throat of hers and strangle the life out of her . . . for what she had done to him.

The silence of the grey dawn was broken by the sharp crack of a revolver shot. It was followed by a man's hoarse shout, then another, and the galloping of horses' hoofs.

Gail stood still, his pulses racing. What had happened? Something violent was taking place outside this prison. He could see nothing. He could not reach the tiny window, but he could feel that the building was being surrounded by men.

Then, suddenly, the door of his cell was unlocked and swung open. A body like a sack of coals fell with a sinister thud on to the stone floor. Over it stepped a masked man. He saluted Gail.

'Come on, Mike — we've got you, lad.'

Gail looked at him silently. The masked man had flaming red hair and moustache. He knew with whom he had to deal. He had heard Mike speak of this man. He was one of the most desperate bandits in the mountains and a follower of 'Phantom Hoofs' — a man known as Red Rube. Gail realised what had happened. Red Rube had got wind of the arrest of 'Phantom Hoofs', and had brought the gang down to effect a daring escape. Rube obviously mistook Gail for Mike — and bundled him out of the cell without hesitation. Gail, only too thankful to be released, questioned him.

'How'd the boys do it?'

'Put a bullet through your guard,' said Red Rube grimly, 'and laid out the Sheriff. It takes more than a handful of guys like them to hold 'Phantom Hoofs'. Here's your mount for you, lad.'

Gail found himself in the saddle of a big, black horse. A little crowd of masked men — desperadoes, all of them — circled round him. They all saluted him.

''Phantom Hoofs!' Good lad!'

Gail played up to the occasion. He adopted the manner of his brother, which was slightly rougher and coarser than his own, thanked them for helping him, responded gaily to their rough jests.

'Where shall we find you when we want you, lad?' Red Rube asked him.

'Cave in the Troit Pass,' said Gail briefly, 'and tomorrow, over the border.'

'We'll follow you,' said Rube.

'Ay — we'll follow,' said the others.

A moment later they had dispersed. The sound of the horses' hoofs had died away. The Sheriff's dwelling was silent and peaceful again. But two men lay dead in that bitter dawn, and those who found them, later, found also a piece of paper stuck to the door of the cell. On it was written:

'*Sorry to disappoint you.*
'*Phantom Hoofs*'.'

The whole of the countryside was in an uproar that morning. 'Phantom Hoofs' had escaped again. Was the man a devil incarnate that no walls or locks could hold him down?

Gail O'Shean reached the secret cave in the Mountain Pass, exhausted. He had many things to say to Mike. And one thing he was going to make plain. Mike must issue an order to his gang that no murder was to be committed under any circumstances. If he did not — this was the last Mike would ever see of him. Two innocent men had died this morning, and Gail — thankful though he was for freedom — sickened at the thought.

The memory of Fenella and her treachery was still hot upon him. As soon as he had thrashed this thing out with his brother, he would see Fenella. He would go to her disguised . . . but he would see her . . . and she should pay . . . pay with the kisses of those treacherous lips . . . those red, passionate lips that had responded to his own last night.

But Gail did not find his brother in the cave. The real 'Phantom Hoofs' was a quick worker. No sooner had the dawn broken over the mountains, and he had found that Gail had not come back, than he had taken it for granted that Gail had been betrayed and arrested. Well — the boys would help him out, as soon as they got wind of it. But he, Mike, wanted Fenella's money — the money he would have had by now if his brother hadn't interfered.

Mike put on a shabby suit, an old coat, tweed cap and horn-rimmed glasses. He was no longer 'Phantom Hoofs,' the fearless rider and outlaw. He was a shabby-looking American, with a slight stoop, who carried a suitcase and might be from the States. He walked all those miles from the Pass down to Fenella's ranch. Nobody on the look-out for 'Phantom Hoofs' would have cast a second glance at this stranger. It was only a few minutes after he had gone, that Gail returned to the cave. But Mike had taken a foot-path down the mountain side, off the road, so the brothers did not meet.

10

Fenella's discovery that Max Geering was unfaithful to her — and was all that she had thought him when, in a moment of passionate resentment, she had married Gail O'Shean — came as a shattering blow.

She had loved Max. Once she had doubted him, then made up her mind never to doubt him again, and she had fully intended to marry him when she gained her freedom from Gail O'Shean. Now she knew that he was a creature beneath contempt, and her wounded pride was, perhaps, greater than her wounded love.

She did not cry. The grief and shame of it went too deep for tears. She felt that she must get away — right away from the ranch. She could not endure to see pity in the eyes of her employees. She had been so proud — so proud of

Max and their love.

She did not ride her horse that morning. She took her sledge and an Indian boy to drive the dogs. She felt she must drive miles and miles away — fight this thing out. Later she would come back and rearrange her affairs. Max might die of his wound. If he did not die, he could no longer stay here as her manager. He would have to go. She had bitter, painful days ahead of her.

Then she began thinking about Gail O'Shean again. She wanted to see him . . . more now than ever. First of all she would drive over to the Sheriff.

Before she had covered half a mile from the Bar-None Ranch she met a man walking along the road. He carried a small suitcase and wore glasses. He was a stranger to her. He looked very weary and chilled, and since he was on her land, Fenella — ever kind and friendly — stopped the sledge and spoke to him.

'Where are you going? I'm Fenella Shaw. Can I give you a lift?'

He looked at her eagerly, looked up and down the road, made sure they were quite alone; then whipped off his cap and glasses.

'Fenella!' he said.

Her heart gave a great leap. She knew now who he was. She looked into the light blue eyes, suddenly warmed and thrilled out of her depression.

'Gail — it's you — then you've escaped!' she cried.

'Yes,' said Mike cautiously, 'I've escaped.'

'Oh, Gail,' she said. 'Gail, I wanted to tell you it wasn't I who betrayed you. I swear it. You thought it was. But, Gail, I didn't give you away. You must believe me.'

Mike O'Shean gave her a sly look. He was not quite certain in his own mind what had happened between his brother and this woman last night, but he was quick to realise that they were not on bad terms with each other, and that she was glad 'he' had escaped. In a flash, 'Phantom Hoofs' made up his mind.

He would make use of this situation. He would get this girl up to the cave in the Pass, keep her there and hold her for ransom.

'When they took you away, I thought I'd never see you again,' she said.

So they had arrested Gail, thought Mike. Well and good. Let him stay in gaol a bit. Mike wanted to play his own game.

'Listen, Fenella,' he said, speaking very softly. 'Since you swear you didn't betray me — I'll believe you. But you must do something for me — to prove it.'

'What can I do?' she asked.

'Dismiss your Indian and drive me now — to the Troit Pass — where I shall find safety. We can go as far as the Pass, then walk.'

'Very well, I'll do that — anything,' said Fenella. For after what had happened with Max, what did she care?

Mike smiled. He threw his case into the back of the sledge. Here was stupendous luck, he thought. He took the dog reins from the Indian and sent the boy off.

'Wonderful girl,' he whispered.

Fenella was staring at him. And suddenly her heart missed a beat. She remembered what Gail had told her about Mike, his brother. And she was not so sure now whether this *was* Gail . . . or Mike . . . the real 'Phantom Hoofs'.

A queer terror seized her.

'Gail . . . ' she began.

Then Mike blundered. He flung his arms around her.

'Little wife,' he said.

Then, in his arms, she knew that this was not the man she had married. This was Mike. It was Mike who was trying to make her drive with him up to the mountain pass. Probably Gail had not escaped — after all.

She tried to call to her Indian driver, but he had gone out of sight.

'Let me go,' she said. 'I know you, Mike O'Shean. You aren't Gail. Let me go. I'm not coming with you.'

'Oh, yes, you are,' said Michael O'Shean. 'You little fool — when 'Phantom Hoofs' says he is going to do a thing — *he does it.*'

For a moment panic gripped Fenella. She held herself taut in the arms of the man whom she knew, definitely, now, was the real 'Phantom Hoofs.' The police might not be able to tell the difference between the brothers. Maybe no man could guess. But a woman, with her intuition and sensitiveness, could tell. Fenella had *felt,* rather than seen, the difference between Gail and Mike.

'You're not Gail,' she said between her teeth as she fought against him. 'Let me go.'

'Oh, no — I want you — and this jolly little sledge, which will be most useful,' said Mike. He was chuckling. He was a fiend, she thought, a fiend who looked like Gail O'Shean. 'Look here, Lady of Bar-None Ranch,' he added, 'go on fighting me and I'll have to tighten my fingers round that pretty white throat of yours just a little bit.'

159

She looked at him in horror. She felt his fingers close about her throat. She saw murder written in those light blue eyes of his. And suddenly she was afraid for her life. She remembered the wild tales which circulated round Alberta about 'Phantom Hoofs'. His complete disregard for law, his many crimes. Perhaps he would even stoop to murder — who could say? Fenella was young and she did not want to die.

She went limp in Mike's arms.

'What do you want me to do?' she panted.

'Ah, now you're being a sensible girl. I want you to help me. After all, I'm your husband.'

'You are *not* . . . '

'Little fool,' interrupted Mike, 'I am. Do you think there are two of us?'

'I know there are. You and Gail. You can't fool me.'

'Rubbish!' He was still laughing. 'There is only one 'Phantom Hoofs'.'

'But there are two brothers,' she said, 'and the one I married is Gail.'

'I won't argue with you any longer. There's only one thing to be done with an argumentative woman . . . and I must do it.'

'For God's sake let me go . . . ' began Fenella. She looked wildly up and down the road. It was deserted. Snow was beginning to fall gently on to the whiteness of the ground. It was a lonely road that led to her ranch, and the cowboys were busy rounding up the cattle. Her Indian driver had vanished from sight. Nobody was likely to pass this way. She turned to the man again. He had whipped off his glasses, his coat, his hat. He was 'Phantom Hoofs' again. Fenella, her gaze focused on him, was filled even now with strange misgivings. He was so amazingly like the man she had married, and whose passionate caresses, that other night, had awakened inexplicable emotions in her — thrilled her until she was ashamed. Were there two brothers? Or had this one man, 'Phantom Hoofs', played with her as a cat plays with a mouse? Had he two personalities, two sides to his nature? Was she the wife of this crime-stained outlaw with his curiously attractive face?

She was given little more time in which to think — to move. Michael O'Shean was a fast worker. He took the girl's wrists and bound them behind her back. With a scarlet, spotted handkerchief he gagged her mouth, and with another tied her ankles. Trussed, helpless, Fenella lay there on the sledge, and Mike, laughing at her, covered her with his coat.

'Sorry to be unkind,' he said, 'but I'm a desperate man. And now — forgive me if I take you for a drive that may be a trifle uncomfortable.'

Fenella lay motionless, her heart-beats fast and painful. Her courage was failing her. Where was this man taking her? What would happen to her? Instinctively her lips framed the name 'Max'. But only for an instant. Then she felt sick to the soul. Max was no longer her lover or protector. He had failed her. He had humiliated her to the dregs. She was suddenly terribly alone. Lying there under Mike's coat, bound and cramped, she felt the sledge move along the snow tracks. She could hear Mike whipping up the dogs. She lay half conscious, careless as to what happened to her now. The man urged the dogs on, and the sledge moved faster; then more slowly. She realised that they were beginning to climb the mountains.

It seemed to her a very long time before the drive came to an end. Then at last the coat was removed and her gag untied. Her wrists and ankles were free. She struggled into a sitting position. With dazed eyes she saw that she was at the entrance of a cave cut out of a frowning gorge. The air here was rare and piercing, and the mountain tops were white with snow. Two thousand feet below lay the thawing pastures of her ranch. But up here spring had not yet laid a gentle finger on the earth, and it was still bitterly cold in spite of the sunlight.

This Fenella believed to be the famous Troit Pass. This, then, was a haunt of 'Phantom Hoofs.'

Mike O'Shean tethered the dogs and came up to Fenella's side, swaggering a bit, thumbs stuck in his belt, which was full of cartridges.

'Accept my hospitality, charming wife — in the only home I can offer you.'

Fenella looked him straight in the eyes.

'I am not your wife, Mike O'Shean.'

He shrugged his shoulders.

'Say what you like. You'll do as I tell you.'

He took her hand and began to pull her towards the cave. Fenella looked about her wildly. She was becoming more conscious of the terrifying fact that she was up here in this solitary spot alone with this man. Alone in this snow-bound, isolated mountain pass. *What did he mean to do with her?*

'You fiend, let go of me,' she began, trying to free her wrists from his fingers.

Mike O'Shean did not wait to argue.

He picked her up in his arms.

'I must treat you like a naughty child,' he said.

Held thus in his arms, she was carried into the cave. They left the marvellous vista of the snow-white, sunlit pass behind them and came into darkness. 'Phantom Hoofs' seemed to know his way well. He must have the eyes of a cat, Fenella thought, in such impenetrable gloom. She could see nothing. Then they reached a sudden opening — a vaulted roof. Here was a rough-and-ready room. A safety lamp burned on a ledge carved from the rock. There were rugs, cushions, evidence that human beings lived and slept and ate here. On the walls hung some rifles, a wooden table bore a couple of glasses, some bottles, and the remains of a meal, meat, bread, and cheese.

Fenella was set on her feet.

Mike O'Shean waved a hand round the cave.

'One of my hiding-places — now also yours.'

She tried to face him calmly, although her throat felt dry with fear.

'You can't keep me here, and whatever harm you do me, you'll pay for if my men get you. They won't wait for the Sheriff.'

'Come, Fenella O'Shean,' he said, half-closing his eyes. 'Those are grim words for such a pretty woman.'

'From what I hear, you do grim things, Mike O'Shean.'

He sat down at the table and poured himself out a whisky. Having drained it, he drew a hand across his lips.

'I like your spirit, girl,' he said. 'I'm glad I married you.'

She put her hands in her pockets and wished that she could stop trembling. Fenella, Dick Shaw's daughter, wasn't one to show fear, and yet she knew what fear was. She was in the hands of a reckless outlaw in a hiding-place which she was sure neither the police nor her men, who might search for her, would ever discover.

'Keep your sense of humour, Fenella,'

she told herself, biting hard on her lips, and thereupon tried to think of the days not so long ago when she played bridge in a select London flat with a lot of select ladies who might believe that these things happened to girls on the films — but not in real life.

'Look here,' she addressed the man. 'You know as well as I do that you're Gail's brother, and that you didn't marry me.'

He shrugged his shoulders.

'I know nothing of the sort.'

'What are you going to do with me?'

'Keep you here for ransom.'

'A regular Tom Mix,' said Fenella with a flash of spirit.

That seemed to annoy him. Mike O'Shean disliked being ridiculed. He got up and walked lazily towards her.

'Out for film stuff, are you?'

She backed away, her heart galloping.

'No, but you are.'

'Then let's do it properly. The villain of the piece attacks pretty defenceless girl.'

And then she was in his arms and she felt his breath against her cheek.

'What about the defenceless girl giving the villain of the piece a kiss?' he sneered.

She tried to push him away with her small fists.

'Get away from me.'

'Why should I? Don't you belong to me?'

And then, before Fenella could answer that question, it was answered for her. From behind them came a man's deep voice:

'No! She belongs to *me*.'

11

The man known as 'Phantom Hoofs' released the girl in his arms. Fenella drew back and stood against the cold, rocky wall with one hand against her lips. Now, in the dim, lamp-lit cave, she saw a slim, lithe figure in riding-kit . . . a man so amazingly like the one who had just taken hold of her that she was bewildered. She stared from one to the other. And a queer relief replaced her terror and her disgust. She knew now, beyond doubt, that there were two O'Sheans . . . and that this brutish outlaw was not Gail. Gail had come to her rescue. But heavens! how alike they were. The same build, the same brown faces, the same black hair with a white, single lock.

'Gail!' Fenella said with a sob.

Gail O'Shean barely glanced at her. His eyes — dark with rage — were fixed on Mike.

'You treacherous hound!' he said.

Mike's hand instinctively went to his hip-pocket.

'Now then, take care, Gail.'

'Take care? You *fool*! I'm not afraid of you. But I'll make you sorry for playing this trick on the woman who's my wife.'

Fenella shivered with a strange excitement. This Gail was different . . . yes, utterly different from his brother. He lacked the coarseness of 'Phantom Hoofs'. And all the romance in her was roused and thrilled by the fashion in which he spoke of her. *'The woman who's my wife.'* Possessively, superbly he said those words in his haunting Irish voice.

'He's fine,' she thought. 'He's got something grand in him. I like him, and I don't think I need be afraid of him.'

Then Mike O'Shean, with a shout of: 'Be damned to you, Gail!' sprang at his brother.

Gail caught the clenched fist that shot towards his face.

170

'If it's to be a fight, I'll fight you all right,' he said. 'I know now what a fool I was to tell you about my marriage. You've played a dirty game, and, by God, I'll not forgive it, Mike.'

'I won't need to be forgiven. I'll kill you,' said Mike in a blazing rage, 'and I'll marry this woman myself . . . when you're in your grave . . . '

'Come outside and fight in the snow,' said Gail. 'Not here . . . you swine . . . '

'No, don't fight, Gail!' said Fenella.

He threw a brief glance at her.

'Wait in here,' he said.

She felt sick. Leaning against the wall, she watched the brothers make their way down the dark, winding passage that led into the snow-covered world.

A sensation of terror seized her. She did not want to stay in here alone. She called:

'Gail! Gail!'

The name echoed like a ghostly voice through the cave. She began to sob under her breath. She knew that if Gail O'Shean were killed by his brother she would be utterly in the hands of 'Phantom Hoofs.' If Gail survived, won this battle, she would be in *his* hands. Well, that didn't seem to matter. He would let her go. He didn't want to keep her for ransom or anything else, she was sure.

She began to grope her way through the darkness, out of the cave. She could not stay here alone or she would go mad. She listened intently, fearing the crack of a revolver shot; one of them might shoot. Death might blot out one of the O'Shean brothers, and so end this quarrel over her.

The way out of this cave seemed endless. Gradually she saw a ray of light and she came to the entrance. Half-blinded by the brilliant flash of sun on the snow, she stood there, and saw the brothers fighting, wrestling near the edge of the road. They fell together as she watched, rolling over and over. She could not discriminate between them. She could only glimpse brown, sweating faces and bared teeth, and hear the laboured breathing of the men.

In horror she watched. They were so terribly near that edge over which one or both might fall to a terrible end. A cry broke from her:

'Look out . . . for God's sake look out!'

'If I could get at my revolver, Gail, I'd shoot you to hell . . . ' came from Mike O'Shean.

Then Fenella saw the struggling, kicking men roll over the edge, locked in a grip of hate, and disappear from her view. With a sensation of horror, she rushed to the edge of the road and stared down. They were both there still, on another perilous ledge of rock, caked with ice and snow. A fringe of fir trees had prevented them from rolling down to their doom. Then, suddenly, a shot cracked out — followed by a man's cry of pain. Afterwards silence.

Fenella could not bear to look any longer. The fight was ended. One of the brothers had won. But which? Was it Gail — or Mike?

She began to run, blindly, down the pathway . . . slipped on the ice and fell. She lay still a moment, half stunned, utterly exhausted. When she turned over and tried to rise to her feet she saw a man kneeling beside her.

For a moment she was too dazed to know which of the brothers knelt beside her here. She gasped:

'Who are you? Somebody was shot . . . which . . . which one?'

'Don't let that matter,' said the man, helping her on to her feet. His voice was dry and curt. 'Neither of us mean, much to you. Least of all myself, whom you deliberately betrayed to Geering.'

Then Fenella knew that this was Gail. She shivered a little.

'What has happened — to Mike?'

'He tried to shoot me, but he didn't shoot straight, and I knocked him out. He'll recover his senses in half an hour. When he does recover, he can work out his own salvation. I've finished with my brother. He is a traitor — and so are you.'

Fenella faced Gail O'Shean, blinking in the sunshine. She tried not to be glad that this was Gail — and that Mike O'Shean had been beaten. But she was glad — tremendously relieved. She said in a gentle voice:

'I'm no traitor, Gail O'Shean. You don't understand.'

'Yes, I do,' he said. 'I'm not a complete fool. I *was* a fool — to trust you. You gave me your word that if I came back to your bungalow for one hour — you'd keep the secret. But Max Geering, this lover who means so much to you, got the secret out of you — and he brought the Sheriff to arrest me. You were a charming decoy. I congratulate you. I was completely taken in.'

Fenella went scarlet. She drew herself erect, but she was miserably aware that she was scarcely a dignified figure. The struggle with Mike had disarranged her clothes. Her woolly jumper was torn. There was a rent on one shoulder. Her hair was a mess — her face, she imagined, was tear-stained and grimy.

175

She had the most feminine longing for a mirror and her powder-puff. She tried to hold her head proudly.

'You do me an injustice,' she said. 'I can explain . . .'

'I shan't believe what you say,' broke in Gail. 'Geering and the Sheriff could not have known I was in your room at midnight unless you had given them the tip. Nobody on earth knew I was coming, except yourself.'

'I tell you I did not give you away.'

'But I do not believe you. You have a lovely face, and honest eyes, my dear, but they won't take me in twice.'

Fenella gasped indignantly:

'That's rotten of you . . .'

'Don't waste breath arguing,' said Gail. 'You've caused enough trouble. I've escaped from the Sheriff's prison and all Edmonton will be after 'Phantom Hoofs' in a moment. I've half-killed Mike, and now it's up to me to get away.'

Fenella, with a small shaking hand, smoothed back her curls and tried to straighten her jersey.

'The sooner you go, the better. We agree on that point,' she said, conscious that she was cross and thwarted by his refusal to take her word. 'And our ridiculous marriage has got to be annulled before you go. The papers are in my coat pocket. You can sign them.'

Gail was silent for a moment. He brushed the snow from his clothes and stared at her the while. She was beautiful — marvellously so, he thought. He did not notice her untidiness nor the stains on her cheeks. The sun made her thick curls look like spun gold. She was as slender as a boy, yet the most graceful woman he had ever seen. And he thought of that quiet night in her bungalow, of the lamp-lit, fire-warmed room when he had sat beside her on the couch and felt the wonder of her in his arms. She was a witch. Yes, that was the word, he told himself with furious bitterness. She was a white and gold witch, and she had cast a spell on him. He had trusted her, and she had betrayed him. Through her, he had quarrelled with his brother and half-murdered him this day.

He would never forgive Fenella and certainly never believe in her again. But she was still his wife. He had married her. They had been made man and wife before God and a priest. She could not get away from that fact, and neither could he.

'Listen,' he said. 'That night when they came and arrested me and locked me up — I swore I'd punish you for what you did. Well, I'm going to keep my word.'

Fenella laughed weakly.

'Don't be ridiculous.'

'Ridiculous, eh? My child, you'll wake up one day and realise that you can't fool every man you meet. You made use of me — didn't you? You fooled me once. But not twice, oh no! I swear you won't do it twice. I thought you were sweet and kind and loyal like the women of my own country. But you're not. You're treacherous and mean. You'll have to let Max Geering know that you've married the brother of 'Phantom Hoofs'.'

Fenella bit her lip.

'I thought you were more decent than Mike,' she said. 'But when you talk like this, why, you're every bit as bad.'

'Don't let's waste time. There's a boat on the river at the other side of the gorge. It'll be useful. We'll use it.'

'*We!*'

'Yes, Fenella. I'm through with Alberta . . . and with taking my brother's place in gaol. I'm going over the border, and my wife is coming with me.'

Fenella swallowed hard. She moved a step backward.

'Gail, you're crazy!'

'Come along,' he said.

'Listen!' she said. 'Let me go — sign those papers of annulment — and I'll give you anything you like — half the money I own.'

He looked at her grimly.

'You want to be free so that you can marry Max Geering, I suppose?'

She did not answer. But she winced. Gail O'Shean did not know what had happened between her and Max. Well, it might be better to let him remain in ignorance, to imagine she was still engaged to Max, she told herself.

Then, suddenly, she felt Gail O'Shean's arms around her. He held her close as he had done that night in her bungalow. But with less of tenderness in his embrace.

'Fenella,' he said bitterly, his face near to hers, 'you are my wife, and you come with me. And I can't allow my wife to have — a lover. You've finished with Geering and with the Bar-None Ranch, my dear. You have only yourself to thank. If you'd played fair with me that other night, I'd have set you free.'

'But I did — oh, I swear it — I don't honestly know how Max found out.'

'I find that quite impossible to believe.'

'Then if you think me such a cad, why want to keep me? Why want to take me away?' she asked breathlessly.

His light blue eyes seemed to sear her

with the fire that leapt out of them. She could feel his heart thudding against hers.

'Because you're the loveliest thing I've ever seen, and as you are legally my wife — I want you to belong to me for ever,' he said with sudden passion. 'I think you're a rotten little traitor. But *I want you.* And I'm going to keep you with me, Fenella, until I'm tired of you.'

'You can't!' she panted.

He looked down into the grey, swimming eyes . . . eyes that had haunted him ever since that last time they had met. Then she had seemed to yield to his kiss . . . that long, deep kiss which he had thought was in farewell. And he had loved her. Today he both hated and wanted her.

'Once I asked you to kiss me of your own free will,' he said, holding her more tightly. 'Today I shall ask nothing. I shall *take* . . . '

She felt his lips against her throat, burning her. Then, pressing upon her mouth in a fierce kiss that made the white, sparkling world spin around her. She cried out in a stifled voice:

'Gail . . . don't . . . please!'

Suddenly she felt his grip relax. But he kept hold of her hand. Swinging round, he looked below him. He thought he had heard the sound of a shout floating up to them. And Fenella, looking with him, saw what he saw. A band of men on horseback. They were heading for the road that led to the Troit Pass.

'Do you know what that means?' asked Gail in a low, hard voice.

She tried to laugh, though her face was white and her pride in tatters.

'Yes, I know. The Sheriff and his men.'

'You think you are saved now?'

'I know I am.'

'But you're wrong. They'll never get me, and they won't be given a chance to get you. At least my brother knows how to manage his affairs as an outlaw. At the other end of that cave, there is a river and a boat. You and I will be in

182

that boat and down that river . . . long before the Sheriff reaches this gorge.'

'I won't go with you!' began Fenella.

Gail O'Shean laughed and picked her up in his arms. He carried her into the darkness of the cave. And once more, in that cold gloom, as he stumbled along with her, she felt the pressure of his lips against her mouth.

12

Down on the snow-caked ledge, fringed by fir-trees, a hundred feet below the cave, a man with torn, dirt-stained clothes and a bruised, livid face, staggered on to his feet and stood swaying in the sunlight, trying to recover mental as well as physical balance.

His bloodshot eyes focused on the dark, moving mass a thousand feet down in the valley . . . men on horseback . . . and his lip curled back from his teeth. He snarled under his breath:

'After 'Phantom Hoofs', eh? Watch me!'

He began to run up the road — choking for breath. The thought of his brother rankled in him as he ran.

'Blast you, Gail . . . I'll get even with you for this!'

Mike O'Shean was no man to forgive a knock-out blow. His brother had beaten him — gone off with the girl. All right. Let him go. But one of these days he'd meet both of them again.

Into the cave ran Mike, snarling like a hunted animal. His livid face bore little resemblance now to Gail's. He knew where those two had gone. Down the river. They had the boat. Very well, he'd have the grey mare, the mare belonging to that little tiger-cat his brother had married. He knew where they'd go, Gail and Fenella. To friends of *his* . . . friends who'd give their lives for 'Phantom Hoofs'. After this fight, Mike wasn't going to let Gail have a look-in with his pals. He wasn't going to allow Gail to make use of the physical resemblance between them. He'd stop at the first post-office . . . the first where he'd be safe . . . and he'd send a telegram by code . . . a wire that would stop Gail's little game. And if he got into the hands of the Sheriff as 'Phantom Hoofs', serve him damn well right.

Mike laughed maliciously as he wiped the blood from the cut that

Gail's knuckles had made on his eyebrow. Swiftly, like one used to sudden flight, he put on his coat, hat, and disfiguring spectacles, found the grey mare that Gail had ridden from Fenella's stables, and rode away.

Long before the Sheriff and his men on their tired, sweating horses, reached the Troit Pass, 'Phantom Hoofs' had gone. The famous Canadian criminal — the man noted for his daring as a rider — had disappeared as completely as though the earth had swallowed him up. There was no trace of him.

Mike rode along the gorge and down the other side of the mountains into the village of Cheeterton. There he left his mount and went on foot. Once again 'Phantom Hoofs' had eluded the police.

In a slim, frail craft, like an Indian canoe, Fenella found herself with Gail, speeding down a swift-flowing river. It was a perilous voyage. The ice-cold water from the mountain peaks ran fast and furiously down towards the valley. It forked away from Edmonton. Fenella had never been over this part of the country, but she knew that if they followed the course of the river, they would reach the Anna Valley — a small mining centre on the borders of the Alacoot Forest.

She clung breathlessly to her seat in the canoe. Opposite her sat Gail, his face set, his narrowed eyes fixed on the river. He manipulated the canoe with a deftness that she could not help but admire, paddling with a short oar, like an Indian.

Fascinated, she watched the flash and drip of the water as Gail plied his paddle. Her heart beat fast. Her cheeks were red with mingled excitement and terror. Where was this man taking her? What would he do with her? She would have given much to find herself back in her peaceful bungalow on the ranch. What would the boys say when they missed her? Would they trace her to the Troit Pass? Would the Sheriff and his men follow? She asked herself a dozen questions which remained unanswered.

She only knew that she was being taken farther and farther from her own territory and the friends who knew her.

Watching Gail O'Shean, she tried to concentrate on the fact that she had entered into a mad marriage with this man — that she was his wife. And somehow the very fact of being with him blotted out all remembrance of Max and his infidelities. What did she care for Max? She was the wife of Gail O'Shean.

The canoe rocked perilously as they rushed over a torrent down, down towards the green valley, gradually reaching the remote dark shadow of the Alacoot Forest.

At last Fenella broke the tense silence.

'Where are you taking me?' she asked him breathlessly.

He gave her a quick look.

'To friends who'll see that our friend the Sheriff and your other friend, Mr. Max Geering, cannot get me,' came from Gail with a short, hard laugh.

'Friends — of 'Phantom Hoofs', you mean,' she said.

'*I* am 'Phantom Hoofs' for the moment . . . ' Gail laughed again. 'Only by making use of my likeness to my brother shall I get help — *this* side of Edmonton.'

'I can soon tell people who you really are,' she reminded him.

His pale-blue eyes met hers in a look that was both hot and terrible.

'And would my wife deliberately put a pair of handcuffs on me?' he questioned.

His mocking voice annoyed Fenella.

'Our marriage was for convenience, and we agreed it should end at that,' she flashed.

'It doesn't suit me to let it end at that, Fenella,' he said. 'You betrayed me once. You won't be given the chance of doing it twice. I told you, up yonder . . . ' he indicated the distant mountain range which they had left behind them, ' . . . I shall keep you till I'm tired of you . . . then you can go free. But if you don't do as I tell you now — *I shall never let you go.*'

Fenella sat back in the canoe. Her wide eyes — as grey, as bright as the river down which their craft was tossing and rushing — rested on him half in terror, half in amazement. That strong brown face of his looked ruthless . . . it might have been carved from bronze.

'Why are you behaving this way to me, Gail O'Shean? she demanded.

He did not hear the question, or if he did, he took no notice.

'Perhaps your lover — Geering — will save you in time,' he said. 'But he'll have to take a married woman — not an independent girl. He's welcome to those lovely, velvet lips of yours, sweetheart — when I've done with kissing them.'

'You — beast!' she whispered, and hid her face in her hands. Not now, she thought, would she tell him that Max had forsaken her, that Max had betrayed her for an Indian girl. Already her pride was trailing in the dust. She would die before she would let Gail know about Talooka. How he would laugh!

She thought of the kiss he had burned upon her throat as he carried her into the cave and placed her in this boat.

'You're going to belong to me and to no other man, Fenella O'Shean. That shall be your punishment — and my delight,' he had whispered in her ear. God, did he mean that, or was it an idle threat?

Gail glanced at the bent head of the girl. The sun beat down on it — turned its fairness to silver. How beautiful she was! And she was treacherous — not worth a man's love. Yet she had bred in him a passion which Gail O'Shean knew neither life nor death would destroy. The sort of passion that eats a man's heart away. The sun, the moon, the stars could stand still . . . but if he held this woman in his arms, he would not care. Let it be the end of the world. He could die willingly against her lips.

That was how Gail O'Shean loved. Poet and dreamer, the lover of nature, born and bred to the saddle, like his brother, and as different in nature as any two human beings could be. They had but one thing in common — courage!

Gail O'Shean meant to hold Fenella in his arms again. She had fooled him and broken her word to him. She deserved all that she got. And he would not die against those perfect lips. He would live. Even for one short, splendid hour she should be his very wife as payment for breaking her word to him when he went back to her that night.

He let the Indian canoe speed on. Now they were in narrow water between grey snow fields and spruce forests. This river was a tributary of the great North Saskatchewan. Finally they would come to Lake Winnipeg. But long before then they drew up at a little wooden landing-place opposite several log cabins. It was a small settlement — heavily timbered, and surrounded by prairie steppes. This was the Anna

Valley, peopled by a handful of traders, Indians and Canadians. And in Anna Valley 'Phantom Hoofs' had many friends.

Mike had described this place to Gail. Remembering what he had been told, Gail moored the canoe and helped Fenella out of it.

She looked round her in silence. It was warm — much warmer here in the low-lying valley than up at the Bar-None Ranch. Spring was quite far advanced and the green grass was visible. She felt almost hot in the sunlight — hot and tired. She pulled wearily at the polo collar of her jersey.

One of the log cabins opened and a big, bearded man, wearing corduroy breeches and a check flannel shirt, emerged. He was smoking a long pipe. When he saw the slim, dark man and the slender, fair-haired girl, who looked too smart for a woman born and reared in these parts, he took the pipe from his mouth and stared. Then he gave a big shout and hailed the man.

'Sure, it's Mike!' he said in a welcoming voice. 'We haven't seen you lately, lad. Treating you rough up country, are they?'

Gail put a hand on Fenella's shoulder.

'Remember,' he said in a low voice, 'one word from you, and you'll pay for it . . . all your life.'

She flushed scarlet and shook herself free from his fingers. But she stayed mute. She was afraid of Gail now. And she did not want to pay . . . all her life.

Gail, remembering all that his brother had told him, made a swift mental revision of it. This must be Mike's pal, Sam Peterson, who was a cattle-rustler and one of 'Phantom Hoof's' most powerful friends, because he possessed some important and useful allies amongst the Indians and half-breeds who traded down here in Anna Valley. Yes, and hadn't Sam a daughter? Mike had mentioned a girl . . . Peterson's daughter. Gail remembered that.

'Glad to see you again, Sam,' said Gail in the rather loud, swaggering fashion in which his brother spoke. 'Yes, I'm needing a bit of help from you. Sheriff and the ranchers are after me. I knew you'd help.'

'Sure — anything for you, Mike,' said Peterson.

Not for an instant did he suspect this blue-eyed young man of being anybody but 'Phantom Hoofs'. It never entered his head that Mike had a brother with such an amazing likeness to him.

'Chenda will be pleased to see you,' said Peterson. Then he added, with a coarse laugh: 'But not so pleased to see the blonde with you. Who is she, Mike?'

Gail's blue eyes narrowed. He put two and two together. Chenda . . . yes, Chenda Peterson was the girl Mike had mentioned. Mike had had some sort of affair with her. Well, if he was to get help from the Petersons, he had better not offend them straight off by announcing that 'the blonde' was his wife. So he said:

'This is Fenella — a young friend of mine. She's had a bit of trouble and I'm helping her over the border. One of the gang, Sam.'

'Mighty pretty one,' said Peterson, eyeing Fenella appreciatively.

Fenella shrugged her shoulders. So Gail wasn't introducing her as his wife. She was just — one of the gang! And what would happen next?

Out of the cabin came a tall, dark-haired girl with a strikingly handsome face. She saw Gail and sprang towards him.

'Mike — it's *you!*' she cried joyously.

The next moment Gail found himself being warmly embraced by a pair of strong brown arms, and a passionate mouth was pressed against his.

'Mike, my darling,' said a throbbing voice in his ear, 'I thought you'd deserted me. Oh, Mike, kiss me and tell me you're glad to see your Chenda again.'

Gail reluctantly put his arms around the girl. But his face burnt fiery red, and he was very conscious of Fenella's cool grey eyes fixed scornfully upon him. This was a little more than he had bargained for. Chenda Peterson was splendid to look at, a creature of the wilds, burnt golden brown by constant exposure to the sun. She had a voluptuous figure, large, hazel eyes, and two thick braids of black glossy hair plaited about her head. She was half Indian — Sam Peterson's only child by an Indian mother. She was as wild and passionate in temperament as she was unprincipled and without morals. But for a long time she had been faithful to Mike O'Shean. He had loved her once in his facile, Irish fashion, and Chenda was his slave. But Mike always grew tired, and lately he had treated Chenda so badly, so casually, that she had grown sullen and fretful.

She continued to caress the man she imagined to be her lover, then her dark, fervent eyes saw over his shoulder the slender, fair-haired girl in her red suède suit. Chenda drew back from Gail.

'Who is *that?*'

'Now, Chenda, no interfering with

O'Shean,' put in her father good-humouredly. 'You're much too jealous and exacting, girl. Give a man a chance. Yonder is a young friend of Mike's. He's helping her over the border.'

Chenda's black eyes sparkled suspiciously at Fenella, but overjoyed to see 'her lover' again, after such a long spell of neglect and silence, she once more wreathed her bare arms about Gail's neck.

'I'm your woman — *she* isn't — is she, Mike?'

'No, no,' he said, to humour her. Glancing at Fenella he saw that she was scarlet, but that her beautiful eyes were cold and furious. And suddenly he thought:

'She doesn't like it. Perhaps *she* is jealous!'

Out of devilment, he stooped and kissed Chenda on the lips. She clung to him, murmuring ecstatically:

'Mike, my hawk, my tiger!'

Fenella's face changed from crimson to white. So that was the sort of man she had married. At one moment he kissed her, called her 'wife'. In the next he made love to this Chenda, whoever she was. She looked Indian, yet she was dressed like a Candian girl in blouse and short skirt, with a leather belt, and she spoke with a slight accent like a well-trained Indian. Obviously Gail enjoyed love-making from this girl, even though it was meant for his brother. She wondered if Gail was not as bad as Mike . . . and just as unscrupulous.

She felt a crushing loneliness and humiliation. Was she always to take second place to other women? Max had put her to shame, and now even Gail O'Shean was making a mock of her.

'Go and get some food for the guests, Chenda,' said Peterson.

Chenda, who was finding 'Mike' more charming than he had ever been — ran into the cabin — only too delighted to prepare a meal for her lover. She took no notice of the golden-haired girl. 'Mike' ignored her. Chenda was satisfied to do likewise.

13

In the log cabin, the four of them sat at a simple meal of home-cured ham, brown bread, freshly-churned butter and corn cakes which Chenda had made. Peterson and Gail washed this down with strong ale. Chenda sat as near Gail as possible, looking up into his face with unaffected adoration. Opposite them sat Fenella, pale and silent, her eyes veiled by their long lashes. But every now and then she looked at Gail and Peterson's daughter, and thought angrily, even bitterly:

'He isn't just pretending to be Mike. He likes this half-breed. They are lovers . . . '

Strange that she should mind — she, who had but one idea in her head . . . to be free of Gail O'Shean and back in her own home. Yet she could not forget that night before the Sheriff and

Max had broken so rudely in upon that hour which she had given to Gail . . . the hour when he had held her in his arms and kissed her with wild, deep kisses that had been enough to draw the very soul out of a woman's body. She had been ashamed, then, of her secret ecstasy. She was bitterly ashamed here, in this cabin, because she was jealous of a half-breed Indian girl. It put her too much in mind of Talooka, and of all the disappointment and heart-ache Max had caused her. She told herself that she would not go through it twice. She did not care what Gail O'Shean did. She did not regard herself as his wife or even his friend. Let him smile down into Chenda's eyes. What did she care?

Now and then Gail glanced at Fenella's downcast young face and he thought, with savage satisfaction:

'She doesn't like *this!*'

The meal over, Peterson and his daughter retired into an inner room. The man drew water and the girl heated it to wash the dishes.

Gail and Fenella were alone. The instant she found herself alone with him she felt curiously afraid, and the blood rushed to her face and throat. She seemed to feel his blue, brooding eyes upon her. He flung away the cigarette he had been smoking and walked towards her.

'I have not told these people that you are my wife, Fenella,' he said in a low voice, 'because the girl is in love with my brother. She thinks I'm Mike. I must leave it at that, otherwise she won't help us. Tonight, at dusk, they'll give us horses and we can ride over the border.'

Fenella flung back her head.

'It doesn't matter to me what they think . . . I don't consider myself your wife.'

Suddenly he smiled.

'But you are — sweetheart,' he said softly. He pulled her towards him suddenly and kissed her on the lips. 'I think you're mean and disloyal,' he added. 'I don't admire your idea of honour. But

202

I want you — you lovely white and gold creature. You're like a lily — so cold, so fair! A pity those white petals are bruised and stained with the mark of treachery. Kiss me, Fenella O'Shean — will you?'

'No,' she said, her face and throat a sheet of flame. 'No — you won't dare . . . '

She broke off. He silenced her with kisses, then let her go — laughing.

'Tonight, under the stars, when we ride side by side, sweetheart, there'll be no letting you go. We'll set out on a mad adventure — a thrilling escape, and call it our honeymoon!'

She fled from him, out of the cabin into the sunshine, and stood white and gasping, her locked hands to the lips he had stung with his kisses. Sheer panic descended on her now. She was afraid of Gail O'Shean — of his arms — of his lips. And most of all, she was afraid of herself. Because she knew that if this man, this strange, strong, ruthless Irishman wanted to, he could rob her of her last shred of willpower and pride.

Max had been her lover — never her master. But Gail O'Shean could master her. He would leave her beaten and defenceless. She knew that to save herself from final ignominy she *must* get away at any cost.

Inside the cabin, Gail stood alone. Through the window he could see the slim figure, the fair curly head of the girl who was his wife. And he was in torment because he could not hate her, and because every fibre of his being urged him to forget her treachery and fall at her feet and adore her.

Into the room came Chenda Peterson. The moment Gail saw her, he knew that something had happened. She held a slip of paper in her hand, and her large dark eyes held a queer, malicious look.

'Well?' he said carelessly.

The girl lifted the slip of paper up to him.

'Do you know what this is?'

'I've no idea.'

'Think — *Gail O'Shean*.'

He caught his breath. So Chenda

knew? But how, in the devil's name?

The girl drew close ... so close that her dark braided hair touched his chin.

'Gail, eh?' she laughed softly. 'Not Mike, my lover. Yet so alike. Gee, but it's amazing. Can any two men be so like two peas in a pod?' She touched his eyes, his lips with a slim brown finger. 'Now I know ... I can see ... you have a more gentle curve of mouth. *He* has been a brute to me. You would never be. There was a quality in your kiss ... something new ... that I liked.'

'Chenda,' said Gail impatiently, 'since you know I am not Mike, let's be sensible now. How ... where did you get the information, and what are you going to do about it?'

'Mike telegraphed me from Cheeterton ... in code. He warned me and my father to keep you here and give you up to the police as 'Phantom Hoofs', because you'd tried to murder him.'

'I see,' said Gail. 'So my brother turns traitor. Well — and why are you telling me this?'

She gave him a softer look and put her arms about his neck.

'Because I find I could love you, Gail O'Shean.'

'But you're fond of my brother.'

'I was. I was his woman. But he hit me, the last time he was here. I never forgot. You would not hit me,' she whispered, pressing a warm cheek to his. 'My feeling for Mike has changed, but I can be a lot nicer to Mike's brother. If he'll let me. Say, Gail, I'll keep the secret, and my father needn't know, and you shall get away safe if you'll take me with you when you ride tonight.'

Gail was silent. Here was a quandary. He did not want this girl. He did not want to be arrested and imprisoned, perhaps, for years, in his brother's place. But there was Fenella. Chenda seemed to read his thoughts.

'This blonde is nothing to you, Gail. You are just helping her over the border, father says. Very well. Take me and I'll go to the ends of the earth with you.'

Before Gail could answer, old Peterson came running in.

'Save yourself, Mike, lad, the Sheriff and his gang are in sight. They've traced ye here.'

Gail's muscles tautened.

'God . . . they've been pretty nippy over this.'

'Into the cellar under our cabin . . . quick . . . ' said Chenda breathlessly. 'The place where Mike has been before . . . '

'Ay — beat it, lad,' said Sam. 'When the coast is clear we'll let you out again.'

'Where's Fenella?' said Gail.

Peterson, busily removing several boards from the floor, looked up.

'Call her, one of you.'

'Fenella,' said Gail, running to the cabin door, 'they're after us. Come . . . we've got to hide.'

Then he heard Chenda give an exclamation:

'What's she doing, in heaven's name? . . . look!'

Gail's blue eyes looked, and he knew,

207

only too well, what Fenella was doing. She had sighted the Sheriff and his men. She was running towards them. She was already well away from the cabin. For the second time, he thought bitterly, she meant to betray him.

'Hide yourself, Gail,' said Chenda's terrified voice in his ear. 'Don't mind the girl. She doesn't know our secret hiding-place. Get down ... quickly ... quickly ... before they come. They'll never get you there — never in this world!'

14

Gail O'Shean gave one brief, bitter look at the figure of Fenella fast vanishing towards the distant figures of the Sheriff and his men. His nostrils dilated. He clenched his hands at his sides.

'If she betrays me again . . . ' he thought.

'You must hide — oh, for heaven's sake, you must hide, my darling,' said the husky voice of Chenda. Her slim brown fingers pulled frantically at his arm. He shrugged his shoulders. What did it matter? Nothing mattered. Certainly he could hide and take his chance, and if Fenella gave him away — very well. It was the end of everything so far as he was concerned. He looked curiously at Chenda, down into the appealing eyes of the girl — appealing to him to save himself. She cared for him in her way. But she left Gail cold. She was an untutored, foolish half-breed, led by her passions rather than her intelligence. It was impossible for him to feel enthusiastic about her. What she felt for him was nothing but the uncontrolled infatuation of the moment. If only it had been Fenella who minded whether he lived or died. He tried to picture Fenella pulling at his arm, begging him to hide! If only *she* had loved him — even for an hour or a day. Even now, in this crisis, he could not tear his mind from the thought of Fenella or of the wild rapture he had felt when he had first taken her in his arms. They were bound together by a queer bond which he knew was a definite fact — something which Fenella might not recognise, yet which even she would discover one day. She might hate and betray him — but another day would dawn when she would regret it, of that Gail O'Shean was curiously certain.

But dreaming was to no account now, when his life was threatened by these approaching men.

'Are you mad, boy? You'll be caught,'

said the gruff voice of Peterson, breaking in upon Gail's wild thoughts.

Gail turned and followed Peterson and Chenda without further hesitation. Another moment and he had climbed down a steep ladder made of twisted ropes into a chilly dark cellar below the trader's log cabin. It was a dreary, foul-smelling retreat, ventilated only by tiny holes through the boarding in the floor. But it was a good hiding-place. Nobody would dream there was a cellar hollowed out of the earth under the boards of that innocent-looking cabin.

Chenda hastened to the kitchen and began to peel potatoes with a nonchalant air. Peterson leaned against the doorway, his long Meerschaum between his teeth. He appeared to be surveying the golden afternoon — with nothing to worry about.

Fenella sped on towards the approaching Sheriff and his men. She had but one idea in her head. To escape from Gail. She was petrified with fear — with the terror and emotion which his fierce arms and lips had roused in her. Her lips were stinging from his kisses. And in her mind was tumult at the memory of his words:

'Tonight, under the stars ... no letting you go ... and call it our honeymoon ...'

He was mad as well as bad, and he was wrong, she argued inwardly, as she ran away from the Petersons' cabin. Utterly wrong if he imagined he could subject her will to his, defeat her like this. She would never lie in his arms, never allow him to touch her lips or throat and devastate her as he had done that crazy evening in her bungalow. There would be no 'tonight under the stars' for them.

Yet when Fenella was within a yard or two of the Sheriff she paused, white, panting, irresolute. Could she bring herself to tell these men that Gail O'Shean was hiding in the Petersons' cabin? Was she going to let them handcuff him and take him to prison in Mike's place — imagining they had captured the long-wanted outlaw known as 'Phantom Hoofs'?

Fenella allowed herself to dwell on the thought of Gail in prison — Gail, who was really innocent of crime — fretting his heart out behind iron bars. Gail, who was brown and strong and a lover of nature, to be fettered and cramped in a cell. For him no moon, no sun or stars, or glory of morning skies or white beauty of starry nights — no aching loveliness and wonder of the Canadian spring. But just prison, solitude, and even death.

She shut her eyes a moment, pressing her fingers against her head. Something ached down in her very heart. She wanted to burst into tears . . . to cry as though her heart was broken. Yet why should she feel so stirred and troubled? What was Gail to her? Husband, only in name. What did it matter if he was Chenda Peterson's lover and if she, Fenella, never saw him again?

Why couldn't she be quite indifferent to his fate? Why couldn't she loathe him, body and soul?

She could not move one step further forward. She stood like a figure of stone. The Sheriff galloped up to her, followed by his men. Their horses were flecked with foam. They had ridden hard.

'Hi — Miss Shaw! Sakes alive, what are *you* doing here?' the Sheriff exclaimed, reining in his mare beside her. He looked down at her in astonishment while he wiped his streaming face. The other men stared too at the familiar figure of the fair-haired owner of Bar-None Ranch.

Fenella looked up at the shouts. Her face was pale and set. She wondered if he knew how insanely fast her heart was beating.

'We're on the trail of 'Phantom Hoofs',' added the Sheriff. 'He's here — ain't he? He carried you off, surely to goodness.'

'Ay, I reckon we've got the devil this time,' said one of the other men. 'What next? 'Tis bad enough holding up the mail and the poor folks who're strangers round about. But when it comes to a-carrying off our Miss Fenella, 'tis enough to make Dick Shaw turn in his grave.'

'Ay, ay — let's put a rope round his neck and hang him to the nearest tree,' growled another man. 'It don't do to put 'Phantom Hoofs' behind iron bars. He cracks 'em with his teeth.'

Loud laughter from the others. The Sheriff shoved his hat on the back of his head.

'Reckon I'm glad we traced you here and saved you, Miss Shaw. Say, where's the son o' Satan hiding?'

Blindly Fenella looked from one of the men to the other. Good, decent fellows, all of them. Law-abiding citizens of Edmonton, old friends of her father, friendly to her. Not one of them but would cut off his hand to protect her. But suddenly their brown, perspiring faces seemed to her like brutal masks. Those idle words re-echoed in her brain:

'*Hang him to the nearest tree . . .* '

God in heaven, they might take Gail and lynch him. Fenella felt deadly sick. The Sheriff jumped from his horse and caught hold of her arm.

'Steady there. Are you ill, miss?'

She managed to recover herself.

'No,' she whispered. 'No — only — I've run too far.'

'Can you tell us where he is?'

'No,' she said, looking him in the eye. 'I only know — he — isn't here.'

A roar of disappointment went up from the men.

'Not here?'

'Then where's the devil gone?'

'We traced him . . . '

'These traders in Anna Valley are all liars and thieves . . . ' etc., etc.

Fenella swallowed hard. She looked at them, and drew her slim body erect. She spoke quietly and clearly now.

''Phantom Hoofs' carried me off boys, but he just — took my watch and a brooch I was wearing — then let me go. I found my own way down here, to Anna Valley.'

The Sheriff scratched his head.

''Course — we believe you, Miss Shaw . . . '

'He — isn't here — I've just been in that log cabin back there. You'd better turn back — and take me with you,' she said.

'Sure, miss, my horse'll carry us both if you'll come with me,' said the Sheriff respectfully. 'But could you tell us, maybe, which way the outlaw went?'

'He left me some miles down the river,' said Fenella slowly, nodding to her right. 'I walked along the bank till I found that cabin. The people gave me food and shelter. 'Phantom Hoofs' went off in the opposite direction.'

'He didn't hurt you?'

'No,' said Fenella.

She was shivering there in the warm sunshine where she stood. '*To the nearest tree . . . to the nearest tree . . .*' kept reiterating through her brain. Gail being hanged from a tree . . . mistaken for his brother. Gail, with a rope round that strong brown neck . . . Gail, a lifeless body . . . he, whose fervent arms and lips had roused such unbearable, shameful ecstasy in her. She didn't love him. She couldn't. He wasn't worth loving. He was willing to kiss other women — Peterson's daughter — or any other. She would forget him and put him out of her life. But she could not betray him to these men who meant to murder him, believing him to be Mike O'Shean.

Fenella was helped on to the Sheriff's horse, and he sprang to the saddle behind her.

'Home, boys,' he said. 'A disappointment — but the man's a devil to trap.'

Without a backward glance, cold and tense, Fenella sat that horse as it bore her away from Gail O'Shean — for ever — she told herself.

Peterson, watching intently from his doorway, saw Fenella ride away with the Sheriff and his men.

'They're going — and the girl's gone with them, Chenda,' he called to his daughter.

Chenda came running out, wiping her hands on her apron. Her eyes sparkled joyously when she saw the horsemen retreating. She could just pick out the red-and-white figure of the girl on the Sheriff's horse. Once they had vanished over the brow of the hill, she knelt down and began to pull the loose boards up from the kitchen floor.

'Sweetheart — sweetheart — they've gone, and the yellow-haired creature's gone with them!' she called down to Gail.

Gail climbed up the rope and swung himself into the room, glad of the clean, fresh air again. He looked pale and dumbfounded.

'Then she didn't give me away,' he said slowly. 'But why — *why?*'

He pushed past Chenda and stood outside, staring into the distance.

'Good riddance to the yellow-haired dame,' said Chenda maliciously.

Gail did not answer. He stood ruminating, puzzling. Fenella had gone, gone with the Sheriff, and had not betrayed him. For that much he was thankful. But he wondered if she was playing a waiting game — waiting for a more subtle method of hitting out at him. A fierce and indestructible fire burned in Gail. That fire which Fenella's lips had lit in him, and which time could not destroy. She had managed to get away today. But she could not escape the fact that she was his wife. He would find her and hold her again. Somewhere, some day — soon!

He swung round, pushed past Chenda into the cabin and found his hat.

'Where are you going now?' the half-breed girl asked, dismayed.

'To Edmonton.'

'To the town? In heaven's name — why?'

'I have business to do,' he said brusquely.

Chenda caught his arms with her fingers.

'Then take me, too.'

'No. I shan't take you.'

'You must — oh, you must — you can't be so cruel — I told you I loved you.'

'Don't be absurd, child,' said Gail.

'You and I are strangers, and always will be. Keep your affections for my brother — the real 'Phantom Hoofs'.'

'No, no, no,' she said frenziedly. 'Gail O'Shean — I've fallen for you. I'm fed up with Mike. Don't leave me.'

'I tell you I must.'

'You're going after that girl — that English girl.'

'That's my affair.'

'What is she to you?'

Gail turned and gave Chenda a quick look and a bitter smile.

'If you want the truth — she's my wife. Now will you let me go?'

Chenda fell back. Her plump cheeks turned a curious ashen colour under the brown. Her hands clenched. Tears — tears of rage, of thwarted passion brimmed in her eyes. She said under her breath:

'Your wife! So *that's* it. Oh, if I'd known — I'd have betrayed you, myself — I'd never have helped you hide.'

'Thanks, my dear. You truly love me,' said Gail with sarcasm. 'And now, goodbye.'

He ran to the river and unfastened his boat from the moorings. Springing into it, he pushed off from shore. The rapid water took him away from the scene of the cabin. Old Peterson came up and joined his daughter. He looked at Chenda. He was perplexed, scratching his shaggy head.

'What's all this?'

'He isn't 'Phantom Hoofs' at all,' said Chenda passionately. 'He's Mike's brother . . . Mike wired me . . . I knew . . . and I saved this man because I thought he'd take me with him. But that blonde girl's his wife. *His wife!* Oh, I'll get even with Gail O'Shean — and with *her.* If ever I come up against her, I'll stick a knife in her back!'

She flung herself down on the ground, sobbing violently. Old Peterson tried to comfort her. And Gail O'Shean, in the boat, sped down the shining, fast-moving river, out of sight.

15

Fenella was at home again. The sun had set, and the strange day — so full of adventure — so full of exhausting emotions — had ended. The cold, crisp night had come.

Fenella sat in front of her fire — feeling sick with loneliness and misery. She had not even bothered to change from her suede suit and woolly jumper. And she had barely touched her supper or glanced at the English paper which had come with the morning mail.

She was home. She was safe. She had nothing to be afraid of. The boys were on the lookout for 'Phantom Hoofs.' They knew, now, that her sledge and her dogs had been stolen, and they were scouring the country for them. But her future stretched before Fenella blankly, and seemed to hold nothing — nothing worth while.

Max Geering, who had once been her lover, her promised husband, had left his bungalow at her orders. Tomorrow a new manager was coming out from Edmonton to apply for the job. It seemed unbelievable to Fenella that Max should have gone out of her life. He had betrayed her for an Indian girl. Talooka, too, had gone. And Tomasso was in gaol for the attempted murder of Max. Everything here had changed, her old servants were replaced by new. The old peaceful, happy days had vanished. And love and all its sweetness had gone from her, too.

Yet while she sat here tonight, by her leaping log fire, Fenella could not stop thinking of Gail. Would he be spending this night at Chenda Peterson's side? She should be ashamed that she minded. But she did. She supposed she would never see him again. If their marriage could not be annulled without his consent, and he refused — then it must stand. But she would not see Gail O'Shean. She would live and die as his wife. A depressing thought!

Fenella was young, and had built up her dreams of life and love. The appalling emptiness of the future frightened her. If only Max had not let her down. If only their romance had lasted, and Gail with his strong, overwhelming personality had never come into her life!

The sound of horses' hoofs disturbed the silence of the night. Fenella heard them and shivered. '*Phantom Hoofs!*' . . . they made her think of the man with that sinister name. Was there to be no peace? Was fresh trouble brewing?

The Indian woman who had replaced Talooka came into the room bearing a note on a silver tray.

'Urgent letter for my Lady,' she said.

Fenella took the letter and ripped open the flap. Her heart gave a little jolt. She knew the handwriting only too well. How often, in the past, she had received the most passionate love letters written in that hand. The 'urgent letter' was from Max.

'How dare he write to me?' she thought angrily.

But when she read what was written, her face softened and her eyes filled with tears. The writing was faint and irregular.

'Fenella, I know I have offended you almost past forgiveness and you must despise me. But I am dying. The wound Tomasso gave me was a fatal one. I have only a few hours to live. Fenella, my liebling — yes — still I call you that — I cannot die without your pardon. Whatever mad mistake I made, I truly loved you and still do. For the sake of our past passion, come to me for God's sake, don't refuse a dying request. I am in a cabin five miles up the valley, known as Walker's Shanty. The bearer of this letter will guide you to me. Come, Fenella, and forgive me before I die.
'You still adoring and repentant
'Max.'

Fenella's lips quivered as she looked up from this note. Max — dying. Max, who was so vital and had been so gay and charming. Impossible to imagine that he would never play his beloved piano or sing his German songs of love again. What a tragedy it had all been — his infidelity — her marriage to Gail — the whole *débàcle*. How could she refuse the last wish of a dying man, and a man whom she had once loved very deeply? He asked her to go to him — to pardon him — in the name of their past passion. She must go.

'Bring my furs and my boots,' she said to the servant. 'And tell the bearer of this note I will be with him in a moment.'

The Indian bowed low.

'Yes, my Lady.'

Five minutes later, heavily wrapped in furs to keep out the cold of the raw spring night, Fenella came out of the bungalow. She found a young rancher waiting for her. Not one of hers, but a man whom she knew by sight. He was from a neighbouring ranch, and had been a friend of Max's. He took off his cap as she appeared.

'Is Mr. Geering really dying?' she asked in a low voice.

The boy's face was averted. He twisted his cap in his fingers.

'Yes, miss. Doctor's given up hope.'

'How shall I get to Walker's Shanty?'

'I've got a sledge and dogs here, miss.'

Fenella hesitated. Should she go? Was she mad? Then she looked again at the letter in her hand. The passionate and pathetic appeal of a dying man. She was too tender-hearted to refuse it.

'Very well, I'll come with you,' she said. As she climbed into the sledge she added: 'I think I know the way. It's that cabin by Four Pines Crossways, isn't it?'

'Yes, miss.'

While she was being driven along the snow track that wound through the spruce forest towards Four Pines Crossways, Fenella was filled with sad and bitter reflections.

How terribly one could change in

this life! One's feelings, one's loves and hates! In the old days, when she had been engaged to Max, it had seemed to her that he was the one and only man who could make her happy always. They had had great times together. Moments of real romance. Her thoughts sped back to such moments when, for instance, he and some of the boys and their wives had come up to spend an evening with her, and Max had sat at the piano and sung to them.

Ich liebe dich . . . Grieg's haunting song of passionate devotion. Her favourite. His, too. And he used to sing it, looking across the piano into her eyes.

'I have no thought but owes to
thee its being;
Thou art my world, and all things
turn to thee;
Deep in my heart with love's
devotion seeing,
I love thee now,
I love thee now, to all eternity.'

Beautiful words translated from the German. Well, she had thought that he meant what he had sung, and she had imagined that she, too, would love him 'to all eternity.'

Yet, in so short a time he had betrayed her for Talooka and dishonoured their love. And in so short a time she, Fenella Shaw, had found herself in the thrall of a passion for Gail O'Shean. But that could only be a bitter and sterile emotion and a shameful memory. They were legally bound, and yet eternally separated. Between them there had been one misunderstanding after another. They could never come together again, and she wanted no more love in her life. She was sick to death of heart-ache, of disappointment.

During that dark, cold, lonely ride to the death-bed of her former lover, Fenella made up her mind to sell her ranch, go back to England and never see Canada again. And while she sat there, huddled in her rich furs, tears sprang to her eyes and rolled on to her cheeks. She did not even bother to wipe them away, and they crystallised in the piercing cold and hung there on her sad young face like tiny diamonds winking in the starlight.

Tonight she must bid goodbye to Max, the dying man, for ever. And in her heart she would also say goodbye to the living, Gail O'Shean. All the sorrow of the Celtic race seemed to descend upon Fenella this night and weigh her down like a black shroud.

She was stiff and cold when at length the sledge drew up at Walker's Shanty and she stepped out.

She pushed open the door and walked in. The moment she was inside that small, roughly-furnished room, which was yellow with light from a smoky kerosene lamp, she knew that she had been brought here under false pretences. This could be no scene of a death-bed repentance or farewell. And Max was obviously not a dying man.

He lay on a sofa by a log fire. He was propped up with pillows, looking white and haggard, but he was far from dying. He was reading a newspaper, which he hastily put down as Fenella entered. She looked at him — her cheeks growing flushed with anger.

'I came because you said you had only a few hours to live,' she said. 'I had better go again — I see you're recovering very nicely from your wound.'

Max held out a hand.

'*Liebling,* for the love of heaven — don't go.'

She found that the old pet name left her cold.

'You tricked me here,' she said.

'*Ach Gott,* Fenella — I had to. I had to see you again. I knew you wouldn't come unless I used a trick. It was low of me. I've been low all the way along. But the one sincere thing in my life is my love for you.'

Her cheeks changed from red to white. Her lips trembled slightly.

'I can't believe in you ever again, Max.'

'Fenella — for God's sake — come

here — one moment.'

'No,' she said, 'I wish you luck, Max, but — goodbye.'

'Fenella,' he called frenziedly, 'if you leave me like this, I swear I shall tear the bandages off my wound and bleed to death. If I'm not a dying man — you will turn me into one.'

Fenella paused by the door and regarded him in horror.

'You're mad, Max.'

'Mad with remorse — with regret — because I've lost you, yes. Fenella, Fenella, my *liebling*, come here — take my hand — be kind to me — forgive me,' said Max passionately.

She was much moved, but hesitated to go to his side. How white he was! Those handsome eyes were wild with pain. His yellow hair was dishevelled. He always had been a very attractive man, and although he had humiliated and betrayed her, and her love for him had died, she was woman enough to be touched by his apparently sincere regret. Perhaps he did still care for her.

Perhaps he realised what a crazy thing he had done. She remembered how terribly lonely she had felt tonight in her own home, how embittered by all that life had done to her. Who was she to judge, to condemn another?

Sighing heavily, she moved to the couch on which Max was lying. Immediately he seized her hands and covered them with wild kisses.

'Oh, Fenella, Fenella — I've been in hell — I've suffered hell. Forgive me — take me back,' he implored.

'No, Max — don't — it's too late!'

'Fenella,' he almost sobbed her name, 'I can't lose you for ever. *Liebling,* you loved me once — be merciful — make allowances — but don't shut me out of your life altogether. It's killing me.'

Fenella shook her head. The tears came into her eyes. His passionate appeal touched her, made her very compassionate for him. Yet — physically she was unstirred. His kisses had lost their old power. Was she mad, she wondered, but she seemed to see only a thin brown face and two blazing blue eyes . . . seemed to hear only a mocking voice that called her 'wife'. And she knew that she would never love Max Geering again.

'Forgive me,' Max entreated her.

'Of course I'll forgive you, Max, but I can't take you back as my lover.'

'Oh, Fenella — have pity.'

He paused. They both turned their heads. And suddenly Fenella went white to the lips. Her heart leapt in her breast like a wild thing.

The door had opened so softly that neither she nor Max had noticed it. Both of them, startled and terrified, looked at the slim, graceful figure, familiar enough to them both, and at the black head with the single lock of white hair. Familiar enough, the dominating, stirring presence of the man.

'*Phantom Hoofs*' said Max in a whisper. And he sat up on the couch and stared at the man in the doorway like one in mortal fear — ashen — with bulging eyes.

Fenella shook her head dumbly. She

thought that it was Gail, Gail who had followed her and was going to take her away again. She walked towards him. With a lightning movement he shot out a hand, seized her wrist, and flung her behind him. With the other hand he whipped out a revolver and levelled it at the shaking man on the couch. The automatic gleamed in the firelight.

'Revenge, Max Geering,' he said in an ice-cold voice. 'Revenge . . . for an old wrong . . . '

'Gail!' shrieked Fenella.

But her scream was drowned by a deafening report. Max Geering rolled off the couch and lay on the floor, motionless. His life-blood was welling away from a wound in the throat. There came a hoarse shout from outside. The face of the young rancher who was Max's friend appeared in the window. But the man who held the smoking revolver laughed softly, jumped like a cat out of the window into the darkness.

Fenella went down on her knees beside Max. She was overcome by horror at what she had seen. Sick and faint, she thought:

'Gail is a murderer. He has murdered Max. It's the end of everything.'

But the man who raced away on his horse from Walker's Shanty, deeper into Four Pines Valley, was not Gail O'Shean. It was 'Phantom Hoofs' . . . who owed Max Geering an old grudge and had taken this chance, tonight, of putting 'paid to the account.'

16

Fenella, in the dark horror of that hour, did not for an instant doubt that it was Gail who had murdered Max. Gail had obviously come after her — had done this thing in a crazy fit of mad jealousy. When she had last seen him, he had held her in his arms and sworn that she should belong to him, and that Max should never be allowed to take his place as her husband. Yes, he had said those very words that unforgettable day on the Troit Pass, after he had fought with his brother. She took it for granted that Gail, having traced her to this cabin, had coldly and mercilessly carried out his threat. It was horrible. To murder a wounded man who was unarmed — in cold blood.

She realised that Max was dead, and staggered on to her feet. The cabin seemed full of men, most of whom she knew. Ned Frith, Max's friend, was holding her arm. He was talking excitedly and loudly. He said:

'It's *murder* . . . he's gone . . . poor old Max. Put on the spot — gee — it's inhuman!'

Fenella looked round her wildly.

'Oh, my God!' she moaned.

'Hold up, miss,' said Ned Frith. He eyed her slyly, keeping her arm in his grasp. 'Guess you can tell us how this happened.'

'Ay,' said another voice. 'The Sheriff's been sent for. There's been murder done here tonight. You saw who did it, didn't you, miss?'

Fenella pulled herself together with a great effort. She put a hand to her forehead. It was damp. Her gaze rested on the sprawling body at her feet. Four of the men picked it up and laid it on the couch and covered the face. Max was dead. It was horrible and unbelievable. There was blood on the floor, blood everywhere. And Max's face was covered from her now. Only a few moments ago he had been sitting there, alive and ardent, begging fervently for her kisses, his voice vibrating with emotion. She had been sorry for him, although his love-making had not moved her. But once she had lived only to be his wife. It was frightful to think that Max, whom she had loved, had been murdered tonight, shot down before her very eyes — and by Gail O'Shean.

Shuddering violently, Fenella pressed a hand against her forehead.

'I — don't know — who did it,' she said very slowly.

'You must 'a seen someone, miss,' said Ned Frith. He had been Max Geering's pal. He was pale, and his expression was ugly and scared. All the men — rough ranchers, most of them — were scared. It was a nasty business. Murder was murder, after all. And they looked to the beautiful lady of Bar-None Ranch to tell them who had done this thing.

The Sheriff arrived. More men,

tramping feet, loud voices, then hushed whispers in this room of tragedy and death. The rug was pulled back from Max's body, a doctor made investigations, asked questions. Fenella thought she would go mad. They made a circle round her, harried her, cross-questioned her, tried to break through her reticence. And she would only say:

'Yes — a man — a masked man — came in through the window and shot him down. That's all I can tell you.'

'But didn't you see his face, miss?' asked the Sheriff. He was beginning to be disgruntled, because she had nothing to tell them and was unable to give them even a clue. This was the second time today he had got nothing out of her. 'You know 'Phantom Hoofs'. Was it him?'

'No — I don't think so.'

'But didn't he say nothing?'

'Nothing,' she said.

Her eyes were large and bright and hunted. She pressed her hands together convulsively. Again and again she repeated her unsatisfactory statement in answer to their questioning. She had come to see Max Geering because he was sick and had sent Ned Frith for her, she said, and a masked man had entered by the window and shot him. That was all.

But she knew that she lied. She knew so much more than that. She could have said: 'Yes, it was 'Phantom Hoofs''; or: 'Yes, it was Gail O'Shean — the brother of 'Phantom Hoofs'.' But she could not bring herself to say either of those things. These men did not know about Mike's double. And she was incapable of betraying Gail, no matter what he had done. She was sure that it was Gail who had shot Max in uncontrollable jealousy. And even now she could not give him away to these men who would put him to death for his crime.

In this sinister hour there came upon Fenella the irrevocable knowledge that she loved Gail. She knew that she *must* love him . . . far more passionately than she had ever loved Max. Otherwise she would have denounced him as Max's murderer this night. She knew also that the reason why she had not given him away to the Sheriff down at Anna Valley had been because she loved him. All the way along she had cared — ever since that night he had come to her bungalow and she had felt the passion of his lips against hers, and the thrilling sound of his Irish voice called her by her new name: 'Fenella O'Shean'. Through all those wild, crazy days and nights during which she had been his wife, she had loved him. He was her man. The man she must love and follow to the world's end.

But now it was too late. There were terrible barriers between them. They were still man and wife. But this night he had stained his immortal soul with a serious crime. It was the end of everything.

The Sheriff let Fenella go. She seemed to know nothing that could help them trace the one who had committed the crime. She was told that she might go home, but that she would be required as an eye-witness of the murder at the inquest tomorrow. She left the cabin in Frith's sledge, shivering, cold, stunned with the horror of it all. Frith drove the dogs over the snow tracks back to Bar-None Ranch. He said nothing, but Fenella thought she saw a threat in the look he gave her.

She kept saying to herself:

'Gail, Gail . . . why did you do it? Gail, why did you do this thing?'

Like a creature without life, she stepped from the sledge, bade Ned Frith a curt good night, to which he gave no reply, and let herself into her bungalow.

She struck a match and lit the lamp on the desk. The room flooded with light. There was still a smouldering fire in the grate. It all looked charming and peaceful and comfortable. But Fenella felt sick to the very soul. She wanted to fling herself down on the sofa and cry

— cry violently with the anguish and horror of her thoughts. She was Gail O'Shean's wife, and she loved him. And he was a murderer. What a tangle! What a hopeless tangle! She felt that she could never extricate herself from it, never know love or happiness again.

Suddenly one of the long curtains moved. Fenella, who had taken off her hat and coat and was smoothing back her fair curls, stood very still. Her heart beat swiftly, violently. Her nerves were jumping. She had witnessed murder tonight and had passed through a terrible ordeal. She did not want any more shocks. She had had enough.

'Who's there?' she asked breathlessly.

The curtain parted. She saw standing before her, the slim, lithe figure of Gail O'Shean. Gail, with a queer, set smile on his face and irony in his light blue eyes.

'You!' she exclaimed, and shrank back. '*You!*'

'Yes. You didn't expect me, did you, Fenella O'Shean?' he said in a cool voice. 'But I warned you I'd come back.'

And without hesitation he came to her side and took her into his arms.

17

A few minutes earlier, Gail O'Shean had reached the locality of Bar-None Ranch in one of his brother's disguises. A white beard, a white wig, and spectacles and the clothes of an old rancher. He was bowed and on a stick. Many ranchers from long distances visited this part of world, so nobody thought it amiss when Gail dropped in at the local saloon bar for a drink. Then after dark, he walked quietly to Fenella's bungalow. But he had found the place deserted. Standing on the verandah, he had struck a match to light a cigarette, and had seen a white sheet of notepaper on the floor, obviously a letter somebody had dropped in a hurry. He had picked it up; glanced at the words: 'Your adoring Max.' Fiercest jealousy had immediately flamed up in his heart.

Max Geering — the manager of this

place, and Fenella's lover. Gail knew him only too well. He had read the rest of the note, gathered that there had been a quarrel between the lovers and that Max had sent for her — because he was dying. And she had gone to him. That was why the place was shut up and in darkness. Her servants were asleep. She had gone to the last embrace of her lover.

'My wife,' Gail had thought furiously. '*My wife!*'

He made up his mind then and there not to leave this ranch without her.

He forced an entry into the bungalow through the sitting-room window. Removing his leather jacket, his disfiguring beard, wig, and the glasses, he waited for Fenella to come home. Thus it was that he was hiding behind the curtains when she came into the room.

Fenella had no doubt in her mind, however, that Gail had come here straight from the scene of his crime. She was madly excited by the sight of him and by that fierce embrace, but she felt a horror of him. He was Max's murderer, and she felt that she could not willingly allow him to touch her lips again; that it would be to her lasting shame if she did. She struggled violently in his arms.

'Gail — let me go. Gail — do you want me to scream? The men are sleeping in the servants' quarters. I can soon make them hear. It will be the end of you if I do!'

He laughed down at her desperate young face.

'Threats don't matter to me, Fenella. You thought you could get away from me in Anna Valley. You thought I would let you go — didn't you? Sure, and you were wrong, acushla, utterly wrong. You belong to me, and I shall never let you go — never, never, until we are both dead and buried.

She stopped struggling and looked up at him in wonder for a moment.

'How can you do this?' she said in a choked voice. 'How can you dare come here like this?'

'Why not? Did you ever think I'd

keep away from my wife?'

She lay against him, and knew that she had no strength left to fight, physically. She only bruised herself unnecessarily. He was much too strong for her. And it didn't seem to matter any longer what he had done. She looked up at him with large, sorrowful eyes.

'You had better go. If they catch you this time . . . '

'You're quite anxious on my behalf, aren't you, sweet-heart?' His voice sneered a little, and she crimsoned to the roots of her hair, hating herself rather than him.

'Do please go!' she said in a smothered voice. 'Oh, why did you come?'

'I wanted you, Fenella, and when I found you'd gone to your lover, I was all the more determined to wait for you. You belong to me and not to him, Fenella.'

Fenella thought despairingly:

'How did he find out . . . oh God, if only he hadn't done that ghastly thing to Max . . . '

'Aren't you satisfied — now that Max — is dead?' she asked him in a choking voice.

'So he died, did he?'

'You know that. He hadn't a sporting chance.'

He let her go, walked to the table, found a cigarette and lit it.

'Max Geering doesn't concern me,' he said brusquely. 'I want to talk about you and me, Fenella.'

She watched him, marvelling that he could be so callous.

He handed her a packet.

'Have a cigarette?'

'No, thanks.'

'Would you like to offer me a drink?'

She seated herself on the arm of the chair because she was trembling so that she could scarcely stand.

'No.'

He shrugged his shoulders.

'Seems to me if I want a thing I must take it.'

'You always do. You're ruthless. Unbelievably brutal.'

He put the cigarette down in an ashtray and strolled back to her, his hands in his pockets. He looked her up and down, his lips curving into a sardonic smile.

'I haven't been brutal to you, Fenella. I've been quite kind — too kind. You see, I'm a bit of a fool. I think too much, dream too long. I've thought and dreamt about you for nights and days on end, and made up foolish poems about you in my head, and told myself that it's only given to one man in a million to come across The One Woman, but that I'd found her. I thought you were that woman. I loved you for your beauty, your courage, oh, a thousand different things which are enough to stir a man body and soul. And you let me down. Oh . . . I dare say I was an optimist to think you'd keep your word, and I suppose if one thinks it over there wasn't any real reason why you shouldn't hand me over to the Sheriff. But I trusted you, and that was what hurt, Fenella. Maybe you did it so that you'd look great in the eyes of your lover. That idea isn't exactly agreeable to me, either. Still, we both know how we stand, now. You're afraid of me, aren't you? You're trembling. And you call me names that I don't deserve. I'll live up to them, Fenella. As you tell me — if I want a thing — I must take it.'

His strong fingers curved round both her wrists. He drew her slowly towards him, smiling at her. She had no words left. She just looked at him with her large feverish eyes. She had listened like one mesmerised to his slow, deliberate voice. Yes, that was what she was, she told herself, *mesmerised.* He could do what he liked with her. It was frightening!

She was drawn nearer and nearer to him, until he bent his head and kissed her in a lingering and possessive way that left her weak and stricken in his embrace. She could only shut her eyes and ask herself in horror why there was a side to her nature which could not resist this man.

'What am I,' was her inner cry, 'to be thrilled by the touch and the kiss of a man who has committed a murder in cold blood?'

But he — not understanding what lay in her mind, went on kissing her — mouth, hair, and eyes. And finally his lips strayed to her beautiful white throat, until at length Fenella found herself, and pleaded with him.

'Gail, I can't stand any more . . . '

'But you know now that you belong to me.'

She broke down and sobbed helplessly in his arms. And suddenly the man found that there was no pleasure in his vengeance. He was not as ruthless as she believed, nor as brutal. And she was so young and soft and defenceless in his arms.

'Oh, don't cry like that,' he said roughly. 'There's no need to cry.'

Fenella hid her face in her hands.

'You'd far better go,' she said, 'unless you want to pay for what you did tonight.'

They were at cross-purposes. He

failed to get her real meaning. He only laughed. 'Sweet little fool, do you think I'm going to let them catch me? No. I've come well disguised. Look . . . '

He slipped into the coat, put on the beard and white wig and spectacles, and became the bowed old rancher again. She looked up at him and would not have known him. The tears dried on her lashes. She felt nothing but dull anguish. She was shattered by the knowledge that she loved this man beyond remedy, and that he had murdered Max Geering this night.

He held out his hand.

'Are you coming with me, Fenella O'Shean?'

'Don't be mad,' she said. 'How can I come with you?'

'If you don't come tonight, then it will be tomorrow, or the next day or the next. One day you are bound to come.'

She shivered as though with ague, and put both hands to her cheeks. They were burning.

'Go now — anyhow,' she said. She

felt that at any cost she must get him away from Bar-None Ranch tonight.

'I shall come back tomorrow.'

'Do you want to meet your death?' she asked.

He laughed and shrugged his shoulders.

'It isn't as bad as that!'

'You seem to have no conscience.'

'I only know that you are my wife, Fenella, and that I want you.'

Overcome by her feelings, she sank on to a chair.

Then she fancied that she heard the sound of footsteps outside on the porch. Wild-eyed — trembling — Fenella sprang to her feet.

'Don't you hear people coming? Go — for God's sake go!' she whispered.

He thought that she was anxious to be rid of him, that for her reputation's sake she dreaded telling everybody that she was the wife of Gail O'Shean — brother to 'Phantom Hoofs.' Not for an instant did he imagine what really lay in her mind, nor dream that she was trying to get him away because she believed that he was wanted for the murder of her late manager.

'Very well. I'll clear out. I'll go back to Edmonton now,' he said. 'But I swear to you, Fenella, you can't get rid of me. I shall come again.'

'You won't dare. You mustn't.'

'But I will, sweet,' he laughed softly.

'Go now, anyhow,' she said.

He caught her in his arms, held her tightly for an instant, then touched her lips with his.

'We'll meet again soon — Fenella O'Shean. And next time, I'm taking my wife away with me.'

Then he was gone. Through the window, out on to the back porch where all was deserted and dark, and away into the shadows of the night. Fenella sank on to her sofa, hid her face in a cushion and began to sob hysterically. The tears came pelting down her cheeks, passionate, un-restrained tears.

'Gail!' she sobbed the name. 'Gail . . . *Gail* . . . '

And she wondered what she had ever done to be punished like this, to love a man who was so terrible as this one . . . to know herself his wife . . . yet no wife . . . to know there could never be any happiness, any peace between them.

She did not think that he would come back. Oh if he did, he would be caught, she told herself . . . and then the Sheriff would find out that he had shot Max, and that would be the end . . . the end to their brief, strange passion . . . and that disastrous marriage — and to his life.

Was there nothing all around her but disaster and death? Exhausted by her weeping, at length Fenella dragged herself to her bedroom and went to bed. Nobody came. There was peace now in the ranch. But no peace for Fenella. Even her sleep was broken by ghastly dreams of Gail, caught and imprisoned in his brother's place — Gail, hanged by the neck until he was dead, paying the grim penalty for the murder of Max Geering.

She was white as a ghost, nerves frayed and eyes tragic, when she got up that next morning. She ate little breakfast. Food made her feel sick. As soon as the meal was cleared away, she ordered one of her boys to fetch a horse for her. It was a glorious spring day, and she felt she must get out in the sunshine and fresh air and ride. Yes, she would ride hard and try to forget some of the ghastly thoughts that haunted her, or she would go mad, she told herself.

Today was the loveliest of the year so far. The temperature was milder. The snow was melting rapidly in the sunlight. In Fenella's garden, fruit trees were budding and flowers were coming through the frozen earth. Down in the pens, the newly-born calves were crying, answered by the melancholy lowing of the mothers. The lambing season was here, too. All the beauty and poetry of the Canadian spring lay before Fenella as she stood on her verandah, this morning, looking at her acres of land. And she felt that her heart would break in two.

For her, this year, there would be no spring, no love, no mating, only tragedy and death. She felt that she could scarcely bear it. Had Gail O'Shean come to her this morning and stood beside her, she knew that she would have caught his hand in hers and cried:

'Take me away — quickly — before they get you. Let us go back to Ireland together and find love and peace and happiness. I love you. I can forgive you anything . . . '

Then she was ashamed of such feelings, and tried frantically to stamp upon them.

While she stood there, waiting for her Indian boy to bring her horse, she saw a woman rider coming up the road towards her bungalow, and recognised the homely face and figure of Meg Pincher. She had not seen Meg to speak to since that night in the saloon bar . . . the night which had been her wedding-eve, and she had received the toasts and good wishes of her friends. All tragic memories, now that Max lay dead, and their love, too, was dead, and all her emotions running in a different channel.

Meg dismounted, tethered her mare to a post, and greeted her friend.

'I've been wanting to see you these few days, Fenella, but I've been that busy with the youngsters. Little Dicky's teething and Tom and me have been up with him for a couple o' nights. I'm that tired.'

She took off the wide-brimmed cowgirl hat that she wore and wiped her streaming face. Fenella smiled at her sadly. Lucky Meg, with her husband and babies and happy homestead!

'I wish to God I had been awake for the same reason, Meg,' she said.

Meg made no answer. She felt a trifle embarrassed now that she was actually in Fenella's presence. The wildest rumours had been circulating round the locality about Fenella Shaw's strange behaviour. Of course Meg knew that Fenella had been let down by Max Geering, and hadn't she warned her that Max was a no-good? Meg and her Tom had not been surprised when they had heard how Tomasso had knifed the manager of Bar-None Ranch because of his carrying-on with Talooka. Neither had they been really astonished when it had come to light that Max Geering had been shot down at Walker's Shanty last night. He was the type who had played fast and loose with women all his life, and it was not to be wondered at that he had come to a violent end.

But what was Fenella Shaw doing, getting herself mixed up with 'Phantom Hoofs' in this fashion? All kinds of queer stories were circulating that she had deliberately misguided the Sheriff and his men, and that she knew who had shot Max and wouldn't say.

Whatever Fenella had done, Meg felt sorry for her this morning. Fenella's face was so drawn, so tragic. It cut the kindly Meg to the heart to look at her. She'd changed sadly since that night in the saloon bar when she had been a prospective bride, radiant and starry-eyed.

'Gee, you look ill, Fenella,' she said to the girl. Guess you've been going through bad times, my dear.'

'Very bad, Meg.'

'Tough on you, losin' Max.'

Fenella's set, strained expression did not relax.

'Yes,' she said.

Meg cleared her throat.

'What are you going to do, Fenella?'

'Sell up and go back to England, probably.'

'Say, we'd miss you on the ranch, honey.'

Fenella bit her lip.

'I'd miss all of you — and Canada. But things have gone wrong — too wrong . . . ' Her voice cracked a little. ' . . . It's hopeless for me to stay.'

'Like to tell me about it, kid?'

Fenella shook her head dumbly, then bent and touched Meg's rough cheek with her soft lips.

'Forgive me, Meg dear. I just can't talk about it to anyone. Things have happened . . . you don't understand . . . Oh, Meg, I can't talk . . . I can't explain . . . '

She broke off on a sob, turned and ran blindly away from the astonished woman, who stared after her, puzzled and uncomprehending. Fenella Shaw was sure in a bad way, she thought, and drove back to the homestead to tell Tom about it.

But there was to be no peaceful ride for Fenella that morning. She had only covered half a mile when she met some of the boys galloping towards her ranch. They drew up at the sight of the girl on her chestnut mare and gathered round her in a circle.

'Wonnerful news, miss,' said one of the men.

'Best we've 'ad for years,' said another excitedly.

Fenella's heart began to thud.

'What is it?' she asked.

' 'Phantom Hoofs' 'as been caught, miss.'

Fenella went white to the lips. But she steadied herself in the saddle and her fingers closed convulsively over the reins. She had stood so much agony . . . she must stand a little more.

'So they got Gail . . . I knew they'd get him,' she thought desolately. For, of course, it was Gail, not Mike. Mike O'Shean was away over the border.

'We rounded him up just before dawn, miss.'

'Where?' asked Fenella, trying to keep cool.

'Close by here, miss.'

'Fool,' she thought in anguish. 'Oh, *fool,* why didn't he keep away?'

'He's confessed to the murder, miss.'

Fenella's face flushed hotly, then grew deadly white.

'Confessed — to the murder?'

'Yes, miss. To the shooting o' Max Geering last night.'

The palms of her hands felt wet. The sweat broke out on her forehead. She thought:

'Oh, God, not that — *not that!*'

'They'll hang 'im this time, miss, and that'll be the end to a deal o' trouble. We've sure had enough o' 'Phantom Hoofs' in Alberta.'

'Where — have they — put him?' she forced herself to say, though her teeth were chattering.

'Sheriff's cell, miss. We've just come from there. There's an ugly crowd gathering round and we want more guards. They'll get him out and lynch him if they can for last night's murder.'

Something seemed to drum and pound in Fenella's suffering heart. Without a word, she dug her heels into her horse's sides and galloped away from the men ... galloped blindly down the white road, on her way to the Sheriff's building, to the cell where Gail would be. She was devastated. He had been caught, and he had confessed to the murder. An ugly crowd, the men had just told her ... who might lynch him ...

The horror of such a thought gave Fenella the strength and purpose to reach the man who, in spite of all that he had done, was the man she loved . . . Gail O'Shean, with the witchery of Ireland in his eyes and all the lure of an Irish lover in his lips.

'I must save him. *Only I can*,' she told herself feverishly.

She knew what she meant to do.

She reached the Sheriff's offices. Her very lips paled as she saw the howling crowd outside.

'Give us 'Phantom Hoofs' . . . '

'Let us have the b — y murderer . . . '

'We'll string him up . . . '

'Give him to us!'

Ugly, menacing roars. Raised fists, men and women too, surging round, shouting for 'Phantom Hoofs'. Max Geering had been popular, and this last crime laid to the door of this famous outlaw was more than the ranchers in the district meant to endure.

Fenella felt deadly sick. Mob-law . . . yes, they could break into that office, into the cell, and they could drag Gail out and tear him to pieces. It was too awful to contemplate. Fenella rode her horse like one frenzied, straight through the crowd to the Sheriff's door. The crowd parted and let her through. They knew Miss Shaw. They liked her. But they shouted and roared for the law to give them 'Phantom Hoofs.'

Fenella, feeling half crazy, rushed into the Sheriff's office. The Sheriff was there — looking pale and worried.

'Is he here?' she panted. 'Is he here?'

'Sure, miss, 'Phantom Hoofs' is here all right. In the lockup. But, by gosh, there's a nasty lot outside, miss, and we haven't enough boys to stop 'em. They're trying to get at him.'

The sweat rolled down Fenella's wild face.

'They mustn't. They mustn't get him. He didn't do the murder.'

The Sheriff stared at her.

'What's that, miss?'

'I say he didn't do it. They mustn't lynch him, Sheriff. Oh, God . . . '

She swung round, panting. The door had burst open and a dozen or more angry-eyed men streamed into the little sunlit office.

'Give us 'Phantom Hoofs', Sheriff,' said the leader of this band. 'Give him to us — or we'll burn down the place and take him.'

'Ay — give us Max Geering's murderer,' said one of the others.

A roar went up from the crowd outside.

'Give us the murderer . . . '

Then Fenella flung up both her arms.

'Stop! Stop!' she cried. 'It isn't 'Phantom Hoofs' you want for the murder of Max Geering. It's me . . . *me!*'

The spokesman of the mob paused. He knew pretty Miss Shaw of Bar-None Ranch. Dick Shaw's daughter. They all knew her. He stared at her stupidly.

Fenella came forward. The strange light of a great renunciation lay in her eyes.

'I shot Max Geering,' she said clearly and coolly. 'I shot him last night to — defend my honour!'

18

The man who had threatened the
Sheriff stared at Fenella. The surging
crowd forcing an entry behind him
stood still and stared. Every eye was
focused on the pale girl who stood
there, with her fair curly head flung
back and her large eyes wild and bright.
Her extraordinary statement left them
dumbfounded.

Then the Sheriff wiped his forehead.

'Mercy on us, Miss Shaw, what are
you saying?' he gasped.

Fenella's heart pounded.

'I say — that you want me,' she
repeated. '"Phantom Hoofs" didn't kill
Max Geering — I — *I* did it.'

'You're crazy, miss,' faltered the
Sheriff.

'I'm absolutely sane,' she said in a
ringing voice. 'Max Geering tricked me
to Walker's Shanty and tried to — to

force his attentions on me. I shot him — to defend myself.'

A low murmur rippled like a wave over the listening crowd. The leader scratched his head and turned back shrugging his shoulders.

'Dashed if I know what to make of it,' he muttered.

Fenella held out her wrists.

'Put the handcuffs on me if you wish,' she said.

'Sakes alive, we don't make war on women,' said the man, and stifled an oath. He was disappointed. He had wanted 'Phantom Hoofs'. The mob was disappointed, cheated of its prey.

'But if you shot Geering, why the devil did the feller confess to the crime?' asked the Sheriff helplessly. This thing was beyond him. He looked pale and he felt nervous.

Fenella turned to him. She was very calm. Her love for Gail had given her courage to do this thing . . . and she carried it through.

'Oh, I dare say you bullied him into

the confession. A bit of the third degree, Sheriff! But I did it. You can't hang him for it. If you hang anybody — it must be me.'

The Sheriff wiped his forehead again. He looked at the beautiful, serene-eyed girl as though she were, indeed, mad.

'God bless my soul, I dunno what to say,' he muttered.

The spokesman of the crowd which a few moments ago had howled for the body of 'Phantom Hoofs' — a cruel bloodthirsty crowd — looked perplexedly at Fenella, and moved to the door.

'We'd best be getting along. It's a queer confession Miss Fenella's made, but we must take her word.'

'Ay — we'd best quit this place,' said another. 'And if Miss Fenella shot Mr. Geering to defend herself, she was sure justified.'

The crowd began to disperse, talking excitedly about this new turn of events.

In an adjoining cell, a man crouched against the wall, his face livid, the sweat running down his cheeks. His eyes protruded from his head. He was in the last stages of fright. He had heard that terrible howling for his body, and he had suffered the torments of being dragged limb from limb before a hand had been laid upon him. When he saw the crowd moving away, he laughed hysterically. He was no coward, but the awful cries for 'Phantom Hoofs' had robbed even him of his courage.

In the Sheriff's office, Fenella suddenly lost her nerve. Once she was alone with the man, she sank down in a chair and hid her face in her hands.

'Oh, my God — God help me!' she whispered.

The Sheriff shook his head at her.

'In heaven's name, miss, what did you confess to the murder for?'

She raised her face. It was deathly pale.

'I couldn't let you lynch an innocent man. I'm a woman, Sheriff. I shot Geering to — defend my honour. You're not going to put a rope round my neck on that account, are you?'

He looked at the slim white neck and shivered.

'Mercy on us — no.'

'Very well,' she said huskily, 'I shall stand my trial — and they'll let me off. But they would have torn *him* limb from limb.'

He passed a finger across his moustache.

'Miss Fenella — you've done this to save him.'

'Think what you like. I *have* saved him.'

'I don't understand. What is 'Phantom Hoofs' to you?'

'That question,' she said quietly, 'I shall not answer. But I ask the right to see him for a few moments before you place me under arrest. I suppose you will arrest me, now?'

The Sheriff sighed.

'It's beyond my understanding, miss. No — I won't arrest you. I'll put you on parole . . . in your own bungalow. I know you won't try and get away.

'Thank you,' she said, and her voice

trembled slightly. It was something in the darkness, the bitterness of this hour to know that these men, who had known her since she had taken over her father's ranch, trusted her.

The Sheriff took her to the prisoner's cell.

'I'll leave you here for five minutes — no more, miss,' he said.

Fenella shut her eyes and braced herself to meet Gail. She had saved him. More than ever they belonged to each other now. She felt an overwhelming rush of passionate love for him . . . and when she raised her eyes they were wet with scalding tears.

'They've gone,' she whispered. 'They — won't hurt you now.'

The man in the cell did not answer. He stood there staring at her speechlessly. And now the tears dried on her lashes. She saw the man clearly. A sorry spectacle, Gail O'Shean, shaking like a jelly, with his face turned ashen and his eyes bolting with a fright from which he had not yet recovered. Was he, then, such a coward? Passion and tenderness died in her.

'I wonder if you were worth saving,' she said with bitterness.

The man clutched at his neck as though he still felt a rope choking him.

'What did you say — how did you get 'em away?' he asked hoarsely.

'I said that I shot Max — to defend my honour.'

Her head drooped and a burning wave of red dyed her face and throat. Then the man suddenly burst into coarse laughter.

'That's rich. That's very rich. Well done, my girl. I like that. And I'm grateful, too. To defend your honour. Ha! ha! ha! That was a good idea — a clever idea, little Mrs. O'Shean.'

Fenella's head shot up. Her heart missed a beat. She stared at the man with a searching, penetrating gaze. There was a drumming in her ears. Then she knew. She said to herself:

'This isn't Gail. My God, *this isn't Gail*!'

She searched every feature of the man's face, saw the coarse smile on the sneering lips, and the insult in his eyes. She knew, definitely, that this was not the man she had married and grown to love.

She stepped back.

'You're — Mike!' she said. '*Mike!*'

'What if I am?'

Fenella put a hand to her trembling lips — trying to fight the hysteria which threatened her. What if he was . . . dear God! She had taken upon her shoulders the burden of a crime . . . of a murder . . . to save Gail . . . *Gail.* It was shattering to find that it was his brother, the real 'Phantom Hoofs', the real outlaw whom she had saved.

'God have mercy on us,' she whispered, and covered her face with her hands. 'It's Mike . . . and not Gail.'

'Phantom Hoofs' — his nerve returning to him — grew cool again and more like himself. He bowed from the waist.

'I'm indebted to you, sweet sister-in-law.'

'Where is Gail?' she asked him, shuddering. 'Where is he?'

'I haven't the slightest idea.'

The Sheriff came back.

'Time's up, Miss Shaw.'

She looked at him blindly. She was dumb with horror of this thing that she had done. She had told these people that she was responsible for the murder of Max . . . and it was only Mike that she had saved. The irony of it! She had done herself irretrievable harm!

Mike O'Shean looked after the slim, girlish figure following the Sheriff out of his cell and shrugged his shoulders. He was saved from a ghastly death by lynching. That was all that mattered to him. An hour ago he had been caught and arrested, and, with a gun pointed at him, he had confessed to the murder of Geering. He told himself he had been a weak-kneed fool. But what stupendous luck that Gail's wife had saved him — believing him to be Gail!

Outside the Sheriff's house a dark-haired, black-browed girl with Indian

278

blood in her veins mingled with a small crowd of people who still lingered there. A bearded man stood beside her. Peterson and his daughter, Chenda. The girl's brown face was ghastly and her eyes were dilated.

'I wish they'd got him — I wish they'd torn him limb from limb . . . the skunk,' she said under her breath. 'He betrayed me. He's refused to marry me — knowing I'm to bear his child. He deserves to die.'

'Hush,' said her father. 'Bide your time, Chenda. He'll pay for his sins in the end.'

'I'll make him pay,' she muttered. 'I'll see him . . . and I'll do what the mob won't do . . . '

Her small feverish hand clenched over a knife in her belt. She stared desolately through the iron-barred window of 'Phantom Hoofs'' cell.

19

'You're free to go back to your bungalow — but not to leave it till we've held the inquiry on this murder, miss,' the Sheriff announced to Fenella. 'Will you give me your parole?'

'Yes,' she said.

She spoke wearily. She was like one stunned. The sequence of events had left her dazed. She did not know what to do, now. She only knew that she had sacrificed herself in vain.

As she was about to leave the office, a boy rode up on horseback, a cowboy, with a sweating, excited face. He dismounted, shouting to the Sheriff:

'Hi — there's mystery after mystery here. Something else has happened now.'

'What's that?' asked the Sheriff.

Fenella stood still and listened.

'Another 'Phantom Hoofs' has been arrested,' said the cowboy with a short laugh. 'He was found in a cave at the gorge on Troit Pass, where he was hiding. Fred Bendish found some o' Miss Fenella's sled dogs wandering up there, and got suspicious. He traced foot tracks in the snow and finally met this man coming out of the cave. Fred didn't know we'd already got 'Phantom Hoofs' in jail, and he arrested this other chap. It's a terrible mystery to me, Sheriff, for he's as like our prisoner as though he was a double.'

Fenella's heart began to beat fast again. She put a hand to her throat. So they had got Gail, now. Another 'Phantom Hoofs'! She could have laughed.

The Sheriff, sick of mysteries, stared at the boy who had brought this strange news.

'Damn it, but there can't be two 'Phantom Hoofs,' Eddy,' he said irritably.

'Sure, Sheriff — there is. Wait till you see. He's being brought in now by Fred and old Williamson.'

The Sheriff turned to Fenella.

'Two 'Phantom Hoofs' — did you hear that, miss?'

'Yes, I hear,' she said under her breath.

'I dunno — ' began the Sheriff.

He paused. Three more riders appeared. Two of them were the Sheriff's men, Bendish and Williamson. In between them rode a slim man with black hair and a white lock, and eyes as blue as forget-me-nots. Splendidly, proudly, his head in the air and shoulders squared, Gail rode as though in triumph rather than disgrace. The Sheriff stared as though he could not credit his sight.

'Mercy!' he exclaimed. 'It *is* another 'Phantom Hoofs.''

The three riders reached them and dismounted. Fenella stood there in the sunlight, shivering with excitement. Her eyes met and held the gaze of Gail O'Shean. He looked back at her as though he did not know her. The blood stung her cheeks.

Then the Sheriff spoke.

'Who are you?' he asked the prisoner.

'My name is O'Shean.'

'O'Shean, eh? Are you 'Phantom Hoofs'?'

'No, I'm his brother, Gail.'

The Sheriff whistled and nodded.

'Brother, eh? Twin, I should imagine. I never see a more startling resemblance in my life. But what I want to know is — which of you *is* the real 'Phantom Hoofs.' How can I tell? I'd best pop you alongside the other and lock the pair of you up, I reckon.'

Then Fenella came forward and spoke.

'No — you can't do that. I know which man is Phantom Hoofs.''

'You know? How so, Miss Fenella?'

Fenella walked blindly to Gail's side and took his arm. She felt him quiver at her touch, but he said nothing.

'This is Gail O'Shean — the brother of Mike. Mike is 'Phantom Hoofs.' I ought to know because Gail — this man — is my *husband*!'

The Sheriff and the boys stared. The Sheriff wiped his forehead for the third or fourth time. He was having too many shocks today to please him.

'Your — husband, Miss Fenella?' he stuttered.

'Yes,' she said. 'And I have my marriage contract, and Parson Jenkins will prove it.'

The Sheriff looked at Gail.

'Is this true?'

'Yes,' he said in a queer voice. And there was a queer look in his brilliant eyes as he turned them upon the girl. Why had she publicly acknowledged him and saved him? What was her object?

'Well, we can't go against that, boys,' said the Sheriff. 'Miss Shaw says she's married to this man and can prove it, and he's called Gail O'Shean — brother to 'Phantom Hoofs.''

'Then what was he doing, hiding, suspicious-like up in the Troit Pass, with a false beard and all?' muttered Bendish, who was disappointed that he had arrested the wrong man.

'I think I can explain that,' said Gail

with a brief laugh. 'I arrived in Canada without knowing what my brother Mike was doing, and soon found myself in trouble, and mistaken for 'Phantom Hoofs.' There are plenty of papers in my luggage to prove who I am and when I arrived. But until my brother was arrested, I had no desire to give away the show. I felt I ought to try to help him run straight.'

'That's all right — we'll take that as granted,' said the Sheriff. 'But I suppose you know that Miss — I mean your wife, Mrs. O'Shean — is going back to her bungalow on parole — under arrest?'

Gail's eyes narrowed. He looked at Fenella. She looked back at him with a baffling smile on her lips. Mrs. O'Shean — his wife! To hear that in public was strangely thrilling. He said:

'Under arrest — for what?'

'Murder of Max Geering,' said the Sheriff in an uncomfortable voice.

'Good God!' said Gail.

'She'll explain,' muttered the Sheriff.

'Take her back to the ranch. I'm afraid I must get on with the job.'

Gail took Fenella's arm. She trembling so violently that he had to support her. In silence — fraught with despair for her — with mixed emotions for him — they reached the bungalow. Once they were inside, Gail made her sit down and gave her something to drink. Then he began to question her.

'You shot Geering — to defend your honour?' he said, after he had heard what she had to say. 'You! I don't believe it.'

'No,' she said, and burst into wild tears. 'No — it isn't true. But I thought that it was you, not Mike, they had in that cell. I thought that *you* were going to be lynched. I couldn't bear it . . . Oh, I couldn't have let that happen. It would have killed me!'

He stared at her, his pulses racing. His own body was shaking.

'Fenella,' he said. 'Fenella — look at me.'

She raised her face. It was lovely and

fatalistic. He looked down into her eyes. They were like deep pools of love and sorrow. Like all the lakes of Ireland, he thought, emotionally.

'Why did you want to save me?' he asked. 'I thought you hated me, Fenella.'

She did not answer, only sat quiet, the tears gathering in her eyes. And Gail went down on one knee beside her and put his arms about her.

'In God's name — Fenella — why did you make such a sacrifice — for me?'

'Oh, don't ask me, don't,' she moaned. 'I'm bitterly ashamed. You don't care for me. You think I betrayed you. You think Max was my lover. You've hurt me enough. Go away and leave me alone.'

'Go away now, now that I know you were prepared to accept the responsibility of a crime you thought I'd committed, rather than let me be lynched? No — not quite!' He tightened his hold of her. 'Fenella, Fenella — tell me why you did it. Is it possible, acushla, that you care for me — that my foolish life is worth something to you after all?'

Her very heart seemed to break with love and longing. She let her fair head fall forward on his shoulder and answered him:

'Yes, oh yes, I love you, Gail. I love you.'

'Oh, my sweet,' he said. 'My Fenella!'

He held her in a passionate embrace, and she clung to him speechlessly. For a moment they stayed heart to heart, his brown cheek pressed to her pale, tear-wet one. Closer and yet closer he held her, and finally turned his head and took her lips in a kiss which she would remember until she died.

'Sweetheart darling,' he said. 'My own!'

Her arms went round his neck. She trembled against him.

'Gail, Gail, what have I done?'

'It's terrible,' he said. 'Terrible that you should have taken that burden on your shoulders — because you thought I shot Geering.'

'I felt sure that you'd followed me there — that you meant to murder him!'

'That was what you thought last night when I came to you?'

'Yes. Oh, Gail, Gail, forgive me.'

'Forgive you? It's I who should ask your forgiveness. I've ruined your life.'

She lifted her enraptured face to him and shut her eyes.

'You haven't, Gail. You've made life mean something. And now that we understand each other, everything is worthwhile. I've suffered such hell.'

He stroked her hair and comforted her.

'I had no idea — it never struck me that you could love me, Fenella.'

'Yes, yes — ever since that night the Sheriff and Max came in and arrested you. You misjudged me that night, Gail. I didn't betray you. It was Talooka — who betrayed me to Max.'

'I see,' he said. 'Sure and I see so many things, sweetheart.' His fingers closed about hers. 'But I shall never forgive myself for all that I've said and done.'

'It's over now,' she said.

'But the trouble is only just beginning. To think of you, my sweet, confessing to that murder. And Mike did it, God help him! Mike's responsible for all the misery. And you tried to save me. Oh, my darling, I ought to be at your feet.'

'No, no — just hold me in your arms — keep on holding me. Help me to forget for a while,' she whispered.

They clung together. He kissed her mouth, her hair, her wet lashes. And she knew that if they put her to death, she would go to the grave with the magic memory of the most thrilling passion that she had ever known in her life, or would know again.

Gail carried her hands to his caressing lips.

'I've got to get you out of this ghastly tangle, my darling,' he said.

'What can be done?' she asked wearily. 'I can't retract what I've said.'

'Mike must own up.'

'He isn't likely to.'

'He shall,' said Gail. 'He's my brother, but he killed Max Geering, and you're not going to suffer for the crime.'

'I'm a woman and they'll let me off, if it was to defend my honour,' she whispered.

'But the mud will cling to your name, Fenella. It isn't fair on you — or on the children we may have,' he added under his breath.

She felt her heart turn over and hid her face against his shoulder. It was sweet even in this dark crucial hour to hear him say such things as that. So sure he was of their love, of their future together.

'Oh, Gail,' she whispered, 'Gail . . .'

'I worship you, Fenella.'

'You don't like — Chenda?'

'Chenda — that half-breed girl? Heavens, what do you think? She was Mike's girl. Never mine.'

'I was so jealous,' she admitted.

'We've both made mistakes and they

291

can be forgotten. It's only this terrible business of Mike and the murder and your name.'

Fenella drew away from his arms and walked to the window. She looked out at the blue sky, at the white peaks of the mountains, cutting so sharply against the blueness. At the dark spruce and cedar forests, at the river, and then at her garden where the warm spring sunshine was thawing the ground, and soon the almond and apple blossoms would be vivid pink and the jasmine flowers would open, twining round the pillars of her verandah. Mournfully she looked at her possessions and thought:

'If they lock me up — if I lose all this as well as Gail, now that I know how much we love each other — it will be too much to bear.'

She turned back to the man, and he smiled at her.

'Shall we live here, mavourneen,' he asked dreamily, 'and go to Ireland for our honeymoon?'

She gave a little shiver.

'That would be heaven, but fate won't allow it. It would be much too good.'

He came to her side and put an arm about her.

'Fate can be kind when she chooses. Didn't she lead me to your house that night when you were mad enough to marry me?'

'Oh, Gail,' she said, 'I couldn't bear to leave you now. I'm a coward.'

'You're the bravest thing on God's earth,' he said, and kissed her hair. 'When you saved Mike this morning, you did the finest thing I've ever known a woman to do.'

For an instant her head rested on his shoulder, then suddenly she stiffened and looked out of the window.

'Do you hear horsemen coming? I do. They're coming for me, Gail.'

His arm tightened about her.

'They shan't take you, sweetheart.'

She pulled herself together and stood more calmly, waiting, waiting.

'We'll go out and meet them,' said Gail.

With her hand locked in his she knew no fear, then. She went out to meet the Sheriff's men as they gathered and dismounted by the porch.

'You want me, boys?' she asked quietly.

It was Bendish who dismounted, touched his cap, and looked a trifle awkwardly at the couple.

'Yes, miss — I mean ma'am.'

'To go with you?'

'No, ma'am. We have news for you from the Sheriff.'

Fenella's fingers gripped Gail's hand very hard, and he returned the pressure in sympathetic response.

'What is it?'

'Soon after you left, ma'am, a half-breed girl named Peterson asked to see 'Phantom Hoofs.''

'Chenda!' exclaimed Gail.

'Yes, Chenda,' echoed Fenella, and caught her breath.

Bendish nodded.

'Sure, that's her name. She asked to say good-bye to the chap, and said he'd been her sweetheart, so the Sheriff let her in. But it turned out she wanted more than good-byes. He'd done her wrong, and she accused him. He laughed at her, and then she put a knife through his side.'

Gail O'Shean let go of Fenella's hand. His face had turned a bit white. Fenella was looking straight at Bendish. Horror piled upon horror, and there seemed no end to it, yet she could be sorry that Mike O'Shean had met with the fate that he deserved.

Gail said:

'Is my brother dead?'

Bendish lowered his eyes respectfully.

'Sure. He died pretty quick. The blade went through his lung, but as he lay there he owned up that he'd done the murder of Mr. Geering, and that he knew that Miss Fenella — that is, Mrs. O'Shean — said she done it in order to save him from lynching.'

Fenella drew a little quick breath, turned blindly and began to walk into her bungalow.

'I've got to go, Gail,' she said, 'I just can't stand any more.'

He looked after her with great tenderness.

'You're all right now, sweet. You're cleared.'

Her voice came back to him, muffled.

'Yes, I'm cleared.'

Gail looked at the Sheriff's men.

'You're all quite confident that I'm not responsible for any of my brother's misdeeds?'

'I reckon so,' said Bendish awkwardly. The others echoed the words. Then Bendish scratched his head and added: 'Seeing as how you're our Miss Fenella's husband, I don't suppose you'll do anything against the law in this locality.'

'You can be sure of that,' said Gail. 'Thanks! and my respects to the Sheriff. Tell him if I may be allowed, I'd like to come and bury my brother's body decently.'

'I'll tell him, sir,' said Bendish.

He rode away, followed by the rest of

them. The horses' hoofs left a fine cloud of white powdering snow which scintillated in the sun. Gail stood a moment alone on the porch, pulled a cigarette from a packet, rolled it between his fingers thoughtfully for a moment, then lit it. He was thinking of his brother. Not of 'Phantom Hoofs', that mysterious rider and outlaw who would no longer be heard and dreaded, but of Mike, his young brother, away back in Ireland. They had never really agreed as children, but they had had fine times together, riding, fishing, hunting. And there had been a day when their mother could have put a hand on Mike's curly head and known him innocent. Queer to think that Mike was dead. A sudden and violent end to a violent life. Poor, misguided Mike.

It was better so, thought Gail. The only way out. But with a sudden flash back to the Catholic faith of his childhood, he made the sign of the Cross and whispered :

'*Rest in peace . . .* '

Then he remembered Fenella, and with a swelling heart went into the bungalow to find her. She was sitting before the fire with her face buried in her hands.

Gail flung away his cigarette, went to her side, knelt down and put his arms about her.

'Hush, hush, Fenella, dear heart. You mustn't cry. There must be no more tears. Life is only beginning for us now, sweet thing!'

She put her arms about his neck and pressed her cheek to his.

'Poor, unhappy Mike.'

'Better dead, my dear. He could never have run straight. I'm taking it that way, and so must you.'

'He looked so like you at times. I hate to think that anybody who looked so like you . . . is dead.'

He touched her wet lashes with his lips.

'But I'm very much alive, sweet, and oh, so much in love with my wife!'

'I'm terribly in love with you, Gail,' she said.

'You've forgiven me for all the hard brutal things I've said to you, and all my lack of faith?'

'You know that. It was just one misunderstanding after another.'

'There must never be any more.'

'There never will be.'

'I've got to work, Fenella. I'm not going to live on you.'

'Will you run my ranch for me, Gail? It needs a strong man at the head of it.'

'I'll run it if you want me to. Do you want to stay out here?'

She stirred in his arms and looked out of the window.

'Yes. We'll share all the loveliness of the spring.'

'There's one loveliness that I shall never share with any man, and that's yours,' he whispered. 'I could never be happy unless I felt that you belonged to me wholly . . . mine, heart and body.'

'I do,' came her low answer, and with his lips upon hers, she felt that life was, indeed, only just beginning for them both. He was her man and she was his woman, and it had been predestined that they should meet in that strange way, and should love and belong to each other while life lasted.

Neither life nor death could hold any further terrors for Fenella O'Shean. The death of Mike had wiped out sin and the slur upon her honour, and there would be no shadow upon the name of their children — the children who would be born of their love. Perhaps here in Canada. Perhaps in Ireland, if they could go back to that fair green country. Who could tell? And what mattered, so long as he and she were together?

We do hope that you have enjoyed reading this large print book.

Did you know that all of our titles are available for purchase?

We publish a wide range of high quality large print books including:
Romances, Mysteries, Classics
General Fiction
Non Fiction and Westerns

Special interest titles available in large print are:
The Little Oxford Dictionary
Music Book, Song Book
Hymn Book, Service Book

Also available from us courtesy of Oxford University Press:
Young Readers' Dictionary
(large print edition)
Young Readers' Thesaurus
(large print edition)

For further information or a free brochure, please contact us at:
Ulverscroft Large Print Books Ltd.,
The Green, Bradgate Road, Anstey,
Leicester, LE7 7FU, England.
Tel: (00 44) **0116 236 4325**
Fax: (00 44) **0116 234 0205**

NONE BUT HE

Patricia Robins

When Mandy's boyfriend dies in a motorbike accident, she is left alone with a young child and little money. So when her son's uncle Jon offers her a job as his receptionist — as well as a home with himself and his beautiful but spoilt wife, Gillian — she gratefully accepts. But Mandy soon becomes aware of Jon's unhappiness, as well as her own growing love for him. Perhaps if she accepts the attentions of Mike Sinclair, an attractive Irish bachelor, it will help her to keep her true feelings hidden . . .

THE GHOST OF CHRISTMAS PAST

Sally Quilford

When a man is found dead in macabre circumstances, reverend's daughter Elizabeth Dearheart is thrown into a mystery. Who is the enigmatic Liam Doubleday, and what secret does he keep? Who is the mysterious Lucinda that seems to have haunted the dead man? As Christmas approaches, and Elizabeth begins to fall deeply in love, dark truths come to light and Liam's life hangs in the balance. Elizabeth must uncover the truth before losing him forever . . .

HEALING THE HEART

Charlotte McFall

Tammy Morgan has lost her man, her best friend and very nearly her own life in a short space of time. Struggling to get back on track, and raising her son Toby alone, she makes sure Toby has everything he wants — except a daddy. Then Tammy's ex, Jason Rivera, returns home from Afghanistan, a changed man. Have the mental and physical scars of both their lives healed enough to enable them to rekindle the love they once had for each other?

FIT FOR LOVE

Margaret Mounsdon

Stacey and her stepbrother, Ben, are shocked when Ben's father, Max, announces he is to retire and hand over the reins of his business to Rafe Stocker — a relative stranger to the two siblings. Rafe appoints Stacey as his second-in-command, an offer she feels an obligation to accept, if only to prove that there is room for women in business — something Max has never believed in. But how does Max know the mysterious Rafe, and why did he choose him to run the business? Stacey is determined to find out . . .

MISTED MEMORY

Beth James

Kirsty Flint finds herself falling in love with the devastatingly attractive Mike Sommerton — but then she learns of the death of Mike's wife Louise in an accident four years previously. As she begins to dig into the past, Kirsty finds herself wondering if Mike is deceiving her. Other disconcerting questions start to niggle at her as well. Why is Mike's son Toby still so disturbed about the past, and why is Mike so reluctant to discuss his wife's death? Could Mike be a wife-killer?